Jukai

The Torihada Files

Tara A. Devlin

Jukai (The Torihada Files Book 2)
First Edition: February 2019
Illustrations by: Emiru the Yurei
http://www.instagram.com/emiru_1860/

taraadevlin.com

DEDICATION

To the Australian bushland and Japanese forests I've spent much of my life in.

CONTENTS

jukai [joo-kai] *noun*

1. a sea of trees
2. broad expanse of dense woodland
3. abundant leafage

1

A THUMPING ON THE FRONT DOOR drew me from my revelry and a familiar face grinned at me. He held up his delivery sheet and pointed to some boxes on the ground.

"Morning! Got a nice big delivery for you today." He smirked as I opened the door and let him in. He dropped the boxes in the corner of the store and placed a few smaller parcels on top. "You guys must get a lot of business out here, huh?" He nodded towards the pile of packages and looked around the tiny room. "I suppose there's never a bad time to drink tea. I love matcha myself. Hey, you're a tea specialist, right? Which brand would you recommend?"

Sayumi, my boss and mentor, was the one who usually dealt with him and I was glad for it. He never shut up. I couldn't recall his name, although he'd mentioned it once or twice. He was entirely unassuming; average height and build with black hair hanging in front of his eyes from underneath his cap. He could have been any man in the street in his plain brown uniform; there was nothing about him that stood out. Every time he came to the store he wanted to chat and, unlike Sayumi, I was not a chatty person. It was becoming more and more difficult to be cordial towards him.

"They're all good." I smiled, doing my best to not make it a grimace. "It depends on how bitter you like your drinks."

"Oh, I love bitter." He beamed. "The more bitter the better!"

I signed the delivery sheet and nodded. "Well, the matcha is over there." He peered at the shelves and followed me as I walked back to the front counter.

"Do you shift a lot of stock here? I've been thinking about starting my own business, you know? Getting out of delivery. I mean, it pays okay, but it's not what I want to do forever. I want to run my own shop and there's always a market for tea. Who doesn't love tea? No-one, that's who."

The soothing mood that filled the store before customers arrived was rapidly fading.

'Go away!' my mind screamed. 'Stop bothering me!' I painted the best pleasant expression I could on my face and turned around. Being rude to him wouldn't get him out of the shop any sooner.

"We do okay."

"Hey, where's the owner? What's her name, Sayumi?" He searched the store, as though it wasn't clear that we were the only two people there. "She's nice, always greets me with a tasty Japanese sweet for my troubles. I haven't seen her around for a while."

"She's on vacation," I lied. "She'll be back soon." I hoped against hope that would be true.

"Oh, really?" He leaned on the counter and got closer. "So, it's just you running the store now, huh?"

"That's correct." His proximity made my skin crawl. The scent of his cologne flooded my nostrils, and I fought the urge to cough.

"That's gotta be tough. What do you do when there are so many customers that you can't serve them all at once?"

"We've never had that problem." Why wasn't he getting the hint? Sayumi always handled him much better than I ever could. There was no person or situation that she couldn't deal with, whereas I found myself wishing a giant hole would open up in the ground and swallow either him or me whole. It didn't matter which, as long as it brought an end to this pain.

"What?" He looked outraged. "How is this place not flooded with people when a pretty young woman such as yourself is at the counter?"

The polite smiles were becoming more difficult to force.

"We're a tea store, sir, not a fast-food outlet."

"But still. Don't you get lonely working here all by yourself? I mean, it gets dark pretty early these days, and you're all the way down the end of the street here, no-one else around…" He let the word dangle at the end of his sentence and looked up through his eyelashes. "You must wish you had company sometimes?"

"Not necessarily, no." I suppressed a shudder. The curt replies weren't getting through to him. If anything, he seemed to enjoy my discomfort. *Hiroshi*, his name-tag said. He caught my eyes and smiled, pushing himself off the counter and offering a hand.

"Name's Hiroshi. We've met before, but I think this is the first time we've properly talked one-on-one, yeah? Nice to meet ya."

I bowed, ignoring his proffered hand.

"Mako."

"Mako. A beautiful name for a beautiful lady."

I swallowed my disgust back down. "You must be busy, please, don't let me keep you."

He shrugged his shoulders and leaned down again. "It's early, I've got some time before I need to be elsewhere."

"Well, if you don't mind, I have to work." I grabbed a book from underneath the counter and moved away, flicking through the pages. Sayumi was reading it before she left, a novel about an ancient samurai war, but he didn't need to know that. 'Get out!' my mind screamed again. 'Just go!'

"Oh, don't let me keep you!" He put his hands up and loitered around the store, picking up random items, feigning interest and returning them. He stepped around the boxes he had just brought in and grabbed a few bags "Hey, what's the difference between this tea and this one?"

I glanced up from the book and did my best not to scream. "The price."

He laughed and pointed at me. "I like you." He

returned the bags and scratched the back of his head. "Say, what are you doing for lunch today? I don't have any particular plans, but if you wanna go out and grab something, then…"

At least he finally got to the point. "I'm busy today. Sorry."

"How about this weekend?" He stepped around the shelf of Japanese sweets and slid up beside me. I closed the book and sighed. "Surely you don't work every day?"

"I'm busy," I repeated. "I'm very busy while Sayumi's away."

"Do you need any help? Because I don't mind dropping by and doing a little extra work if you need it. You don't even have to pay me. I'll do it out of the goodness of my own heart." He might as well have patted himself on the back for that one. It was all I could do not to sneer.

"No, thank you. I'm fine. And you really should get back to work. I have some things I need to do out back as well. I wouldn't want you to feel left alone out here."

That was the wrong thing to say because his grin grew even larger. "Do you need any help back there? I played a lot of soccer at university and I like to keep fit." He held his arm up and patted it. "Delivery work is heavy, but it builds a lot of muscle, there's nothing too big that I can't carry!"

I bit my tongue. "No, sir. Thank you. Thank you for the delivery, but I really must get back to work now."

He nodded a few times and clapped his hands together. "Okay, sure, I can tell when I'm not wanted." He looked around the room and back towards the door. "Sure is dark in here, isn't it? And cold. Don't you feel it too?"

"I'm used to it."

"Huh. I hate the cold. You're lucky. Well, I enjoyed our chat. Let's do it again sometime!"

I painted one last forced smile on my lips. "Goodbye."

"Oh!" He stopped and turned around, pulling out a piece of paper and a pen. He scribbled something and put it down on the counter. "My number. In case you change your mind."

He held a hand up and the doorbell tinkled as he left. I let out the breath I didn't realise I was holding and returned Sayumi's book to its place.

Where are you, Sayumi? Hurry back. Please.

2

I OPENED THE TOP BOX and a glittering teapot caught my eye. I inspected it closer, running my fingers over the design. Cherry blossoms; Sayumi‘s favourite. She would love it. A pang filled my chest and I pushed it away. I dug through the box and removed the teacups that accompanied it and sat them on the bench. They were stock for the store, but I didn’t have the heart to put them out. Sayumi loved cherry blossoms. I envisioned the look on her face when she returned from her work trip and saw them sitting on the counter, waiting for her. That pang again.

Where was she?

Two weeks earlier Sayumi left without word of where she was going or what she was doing. “Take care of the store for me,” she said on her way out. “I’ll be back in a few weeks. Don’t look for me, okay? Promise me.”

I nodded and she disappeared into the rain. There

had been no word of her since. Sayumi often left on side jobs and didn't return for days or weeks at a time. I didn't ask and she didn't tell. I picked up the cup and stared at it under the faint ceiling lights. Exquisite craftsmanship. Sayumi would love it. No, I couldn't sell it. This unfamiliar item I had discovered in a storage box was now a link to my mentor. It awaited her return, like I did. There was no way she would let us down.

I unpacked the rest of the box and set the items on the shelves. Matsuda Tea and Sweets. A quaint little store on the edge of a quaint little town in the middle of nowhere. The villagers liked their tea bitter and their sweets a little less so. That summed up the atmosphere, too. Not a soul in the store. Just me and a bunch of tea bags and tea cups. Sometimes it felt like the walls were closing in on me, and that sensation only worsened in Sayumi's absence.

Soft rain drizzled outside and the overhead light flickered. Again? Three lights in a week. I made a mental note to call the electrician and grabbed the store ladder from the back. It wobbled as I stepped up, and shadows materialised in the dark corners of the room as I climbed. I ignored them and changed the bulb as quickly as I could. I climbed down and flicked the switch; light roared to life, filling the store with a warming glow.

The computer on the front desk buzzed, joining the drizzle of rain on the storefront window. It was a decrepit old thing Sayumi had picked up a few years earlier when it was already ancient. The sound was both comforting and off-putting. It reminded me that I was alone, but it was better than complete silence.

"I'll be back in a few weeks. Don't look for me, okay?"

I wrapped the teapot and matching cups in bubble wrap and placed them under the register. The deep grooves and stains in the hardwood counter Sayumi used as a front desk told of stories older than I, of things it had seen and could never explain again. And yet, unlike most products sold nowadays, it was sturdy and it was solid. It could take a sledgehammer and crack, but not give way. How could I find such strength? Sayumi's absence filled the store with bogeymen at every turn, monsters in every shadow, watchful eyes in every crack. There was nobody there but me, I told myself, but that just made it even worse.

The doorbell tinkled and a middle-aged man walked into the store.

"Welcome!" I smiled and bowed my head. He shook the rain from his thinning hair, nodded in return, and silently filled his arms with tea.

"Hey, do you have any of those sweet bean cakes?" he called out across the store, searching high and low for his prize.

"We have several, sir. Which type are you after?"

"They're about, oh, this big—" he demonstrated with his hand, dropping a few bags of tea at the same time "-and they're shaped like tiny sea shells. My… my little girl loves them."

I stepped around the counter and walked over to the other side of the store. "Do you mean these?" I held a bag up for him. His face lit up and he nodded enthusiastically.

“Yes, yes! Those! I’ll take two.”

I grabbed two packets, and he dumped the bags of tea on the counter.

“Sencha.” I smiled and scanned through the items. “A wonderful choice. It’s Ms Matsuda’s favourite as well.” Sencha was the first tea she served me when she took me in off the streets, so it held an especially important meaning to me.

“I’m not a big fan,” the man said, pulling several bills out of his wallet, “but my wife loves it. You know what they say, happy wife, happy life, or something like that.” He attempted to grin, but he looked like someone was punching him in the stomach.

“I suppose that would be true, yes. That’ll be 4,569 yen altogether.”

The man put the notes down and slid them across the hardwood counter. He threw everything into his bag as I presented his change.

“I hope your daughter enjoys the cakes,” I said and bowed my head. Again he grimaced, as though I was the one doing the punching, and nodded in return.

“I, yeah. Hopefully. That would be nice.” He nodded again and fled the store, lifting his jacket to the rain and turning down the street. His wallet stared back at me from the counter.

“Oh no… Sir!” I picked it up and ran to the door. Rain pelted me in the face and a strong wind howled through the new opening it had found. The man was nowhere to be seen. The street was empty, much like the store, and it wasn't hard to imagine that I was the only person left in the entire town, small as it was. Just me, the rain, some tea and a bunch of apparitions waiting to drag me into the darkness. I closed my eyes and shook my head. The man would be back when he realised he forgot his wallet. Chasing him through town would be pointless.

I went back inside and wiped the water from my face. A photo slid out of the wallet and landed on the floor, fluttering like a leaf on the wind. A small girl of roughly nine or ten years stared back at me, smiling. I leant down to pick it up. My head exploded in pain and the world went white.

Trees. Darkness. Footsteps. Chimes. Rope. Fear. Panic.

I let go of the photo and grabbed my head. It was like someone was hammering train spikes directly into my brain and it took me a few moments to recover. The little girl stared back at me from the floor. My hands shaking, I grabbed the shelves next to me and pushed myself up on wobbly feet, returning to the counter for my gloves. I put them on and stumbled back to the photo. I knew it was safe to pick up with my gloves, but I hesitated regardless. The throbbing in my head continued, and tiny pricks of light dotted the edges of my vision. It made no sense.

On the day Sayumi took me in she called me a 'finder.' I didn't know what that meant, but she explained that I was able to see the hidden connection between things. "Everything is connected, and when something gets lost, people like you are able to find it again. Nothing is ever truly gone. A small trace always remains. Always."

I picked the photo up. No head exploding visions. No overwhelming urge to vomit. Nothing. It was a regular photo of a happy little girl, safe in my gloved hands. I put it back in the man's wallet and waited for the dizziness to pass. Under Sayumi's teachings, I was able to focus on an object or person through something connected to them and find them. A piece of clothing, their favourite perfume, or even a simple photo would do it. It took incredible effort and every single time it terrified the living daylights out of me, but never before had it happened just by picking something up.

Well, no, that was a lie. Under Sayumi's tutelage it had never happened, but when I first discovered that I could see things, it almost drove me insane. Every single little thing drew me in. Pulled me into the darkness. Showed me things I didn't want to see. Showed me to things that…

I shook my head of the memories and put the man's wallet down on the counter. He would return for it when he realised it was missing. All would be fine.

The store was silent. The little girl's happy face burned at me through the wallet's leather lining.

3

THE FIRST FLOOR OF MATSUDA Tea and Sweets functioned as the storefront while the second floor was our living quarters. I climbed the stairs, dragging my feet as sleep threatened to claim me right then and there. The building had been in Sayumi's family for generations, and I was the first non-family member to live there. That fact wasn't lost on me.

Sayumi's room stared back at me from the stairs, the first room on the right. She left the door open when she took off and darkness filled the room. The rain outside had stopped and a sliver of moonlight filtered through the curtains. The bed was immaculate, and all the papers and files on the desk next to it were neat and orderly. Just how she liked it. A fresh stab of pain pierced my heart when I saw the photo beneath the window. A picture of Sayumi and myself at my coming of age ceremony, a year after she took me in off the streets. She paid for the kimono herself; not a rental, either. She outright bought a new one designed especially for me. "Don't you think the pink brings out the colour in your cheeks?" she said. I didn't know what to say, so I just bowed my head in thanks and that was enough for her. She always knew how I felt without having to say anything. A good thing, because I wasn't the most chatty teenager.

I hadn't been in Sayumi's room since she left. She asked me not to, and I had no plans to disrespect her wishes. I walked past it every night to go to bed, and every night it reminded me that she wasn't there. That she was gone. That the one person who could help me with this skill I possessed was no longer there to drag me out of the darkness. It would consume me; it was only a matter of time, and she wouldn't be there to stop it.

Something crashed and I jumped. The picture frame fell forward, flat on the desk. I stuck my head through the door frame, just enough to get a good look inside, but there was nothing there. The lone window was closed and outside was still. There was, of course, nobody in the room either. The frame fell over by itself. Only it was never by itself. There was always a very good reason why seemingly random events like a TV turning on, a curtain billowing with no wind, or a photo frame falling over with no external help occurred.

Something was inviting me in. Beckoning me into the forbidden. Sayumi's room was her sanctuary, her respite from the world. The picture frame stared back at me, silent and lying on its face. Come in. Pick me up. You know you want to.

Sayumi wouldn't be pleased with such disorder. She won't know that you did it. It's not like you're snooping around her stuff without her approval. You're just fixing a single little photo frame. Come in. Pick it up. Make it right. What's there to be worried about?

My mouth grew dry and I licked my lips. I shook my head, over and over, my hair covering my eyes as I did so. "No. I promised," I said to no-one in particular. Hair hid the room from my vision, and I hurried to my own room with my head down. I feared what I might see out the corner of my eye, watching me as I passed by. I also feared what I might not see. Was it truly the thought of spirits that terrified me, or the thought that there was nothing at all? That I was, after all, truly alone. That the photo frame really did fall over because of a minor tremor, or a fault in the building's workmanship that caused it to lean, bit by bit, until finally it toppled over on its own.

I flopped down on the bed and buried my face in my pillow. The room was large and sparse. I had little need for possessions, and aside from the bed and desk that Sayumi supplied me with, the room was empty. Well, not entirely empty. A few books were piled high in the corner, unread and forgotten. Perhaps one day when I had a little less on my mind. I didn't exactly need help being transported to worlds and stories that weren't my own. That I had down pat already.

I closed my eyes and images of the forest flashed before them once more. I sat up in shock and shook my head, trying to fling them from my mind.

Sayumi had trained me only to pick up images from an object upon will. It helped to "keep the darkness from pulling you in again... or finding you out here." Three solid years I had trained under her tutelage, and never again did I experience something like that day... the day they ruined my life. So why now? Why that girl? Why when Sayumi wasn't here to help?

Why?

I sat down at the desk and pulled out my diary. The initial dates were close together, then slowly began to space out. The date on the last page was from a few weeks earlier. I turned to the next blank page and grabbed a pen.

Note for Sayumi: It happened again today when I picked up a photo of a young girl. A customer left his wallet behind, and when I picked the picture up, it dragged me in. I saw a forest—I don't know which—and rope. I also heard chimes, but they sounded distant. It happened unconsciously, the moment I picked the photo up. What could it mean?

I closed the book and took a deep breath. Sayumi would know what to do when she got back. I just had to hold out a little longer.

I crawled back into bed and closed my eyes. It was the end of a long day and I was ready to forget about everything. The phone rang and drew me from my happy thoughts. I wanted to laugh at the absurdity, but part of me held out hope that each time it might be her, even if it was just to let me know that she was okay and she'd be back soon. I dragged myself downstairs to the break room and picked the phone up before it stopped ringing.

"Hello? Matsuda Tea and Sweets."

"Hello? Oh, thank goodness. I was worried you wouldn't be open this late." It was a man's voice.

"We're not, sir."

"Oh. I'm sorry. Uh, my name is Takeshi. I was in the store today picking up some of those sweet bean cakes for my daughter."

Ah.

"I think I left my wallet in the store. I couldn't find it when I got home, and that was the only place I went other than work today."

"Yes, sir. We still have your wallet here."

The sigh of relief was audible from the other end.

"Oh, thank goodness, thank goodness. Um, It's a little late to be coming around right now, but I'll be around first thing in the morning to pick it up, if that's okay?"

"Of course, sir. The store opens at 8, but if you knock, I'll be able to bring your wallet out for you."

I hated being close to the storefront at night. The entire front wall was glass from the waist up, but there were no curtains to shield from the outside world after work hours. The store sat at the end of an isolated little street, so there were no street lights either. Shadows danced in the moonlight, and at times it was difficult to distinguish them from the real shadows that lurked. Waiting for me to notice them. We weren't to go into the store after dark. Sayumi never told me why and I never questioned her. If Sayumi said so, that was enough. There was something not right there; that much I could sense myself. I didn't need to find out what exactly.

"Excellent, thank you! Oh, you're a lifesaver. I'll be there first thing! Wait, no, that's right, I have that thing to do tomorrow morning. Um, I'll be there around lunch, so please keep it for me!"

He hung up and I replaced the receiver. An ancient clock on the other side of the wall ticked… and ticked… I turned and ran back upstairs, my head hidden from Sayumi's room as I passed. Not tonight. Whoever wanted my attention would have to wait until another time.

4

A YOUNG MAN WALKED AROUND the store, picking up random bags of tea and returning them, then picking up sweets and reading the ingredients before putting them back too. He scratched his neck and looked at the large antique clock above the counter. When he saw me looking at him, he averted his gaze entirely.

"Do you need some help, sir?"

Rain drizzled outside, and the radio played some classical music that Sayumi liked. I was never a fan, but it was better than silence.

"No, no. I'm good." He picked up a few bags of tea at random, then loaded his arms with sweets and dropped them all on the counter. "Uh, I'll take these."

"Certainly, sir." I scanned the items, one by one, as he shifted from foot to foot, looking around like the bogeyman was about to jump out and get him. Maybe he was like me. Maybe he knew how much truth lay in those words.

"Sure has been a lot of rain lately, huh?" The weather was my best and only attempt at making conversation. It was like pulling teeth from a stone, but making the customer feel comfortable was part of the service. I hated making conversation. It was never a skill I developed as a child, but crawling into a hole to die in silence wouldn't do me any good either. My mother said something like that to me when I was younger. Before…

"What? Oh, yeah, sure. Rain. Sucks, huh? Haha."

I scanned the last item and placed it in a bag. "That'll be 6,498 yen."

His eyes widened like he was only just realising how much he'd put down on the counter, but he pulled his wallet out and pushed the bills across. I gave him his change, and he pushed a photo of a young woman towards me, a necklace sitting on top.

"I'm sorry, what's this?"

Again he scratched his neck and shrugged. The man appeared to be in his mid-20s, but his actions screamed of a teenage boy who wanted something he was unsure of how to ask for.

"I, uh, I heard this was the place to come to when you want to find something."

I tilted my head and bit my lip to stop anything unwanted from getting out. "Where did you hear that from, sir?"

That shrug again. "Just a friend. Is it true? Do you, uh, find things?" His eyebrows raised in unison with his voice.

"I'm sorry, but we don't—"

"T-This is my girlfriend." He pushed the photo with the necklace on it closer, desperation in his eyes. He withdrew his hand as though fearful a snake might strike it and ran it through his hair again. "I need you to… She's been missing. For two weeks now. I just…" The words came out in a jumble, and he clenched his fists so as not to hit himself in the head with them. "I just want to find her. I want to know where she is."

A pretty girl stared back at me from the photo. Round eyes and a cheerful smile. She wouldn't be out of place in a pop group. A tiny silver dolphin hung from the end of the necklace. It was the same one she was wearing in the photo.

The room seemed to grow dark around me. The walls closed in, the roof pressed down on me, and the floor buckled and swayed. It was pushing me towards the photo, urging me to pick it up. To touch it. To open up to them. To let them in.

"I-I'm sorry, sir, but you have the wrong place. As you can see, we sell tea and sweets. That's all." I forced a smile upon my lips as best I could, unable to drag my eyes away from the photo.

"N-No, but…" The man pulled a piece of paper out of his pocket, dropping it on the floor before hastily picking it back up. "This is Matsuda Tea and Sweets, right?" He turned and looked back at the entrance. "I could have sworn that's what it said on the sign out front."

Desperation poured off him in waves. It pained me to shake my head, but I couldn't help him. Not alone. Not now.

"We don't offer that service anymore," I said. He looked at me confused, and then the light in his eyes dimmed.

"Is that so?"

The look on his face broke my heart, but there was nothing I could do. Without Sayumi, it was impossible. If I tried to help this man, if I used the necklace he pushed in my direction, I would open myself up, and it wasn't a one-way street. I couldn't do it without Sayumi. It would swallow me whole.

"I'm sorry."

He nodded his head, like he knew it was hopeless all along. I pushed the photo and necklace back with a gloved hand. He stared at them for a moment, then the glove, then at me.

"Keep them. Just in case you change your mind, or restart that service again, or, whatever."

I opened my mouth to respond but there were no words that would console him, and I didn't want to reject him a second time. Instead, I smiled and bowed my head slightly.

"S-She's… she's my fiancee," he said. "I just want her back. My name's Yasu, by the way."

His shoulders drooped as he exited the store, and another man entered at the same time. It was the man from the day before. The man who forgot his wallet.

"Welcome." I bowed my head and took the photo and necklace, putting them under the counter and bringing out the man's wallet. His face lit up when he saw it.

"Oh, thank goodness. I was looking everywhere for it, and then my wife went into a panic and, let me tell you, it's never a good time when that happens."

I handed it to him and smiled. "Of course, sir. I'm glad we were able to return it safely to you."

He held it up and smiled and made his way towards the door.

"Um, sir." I didn't want to get involved, but the words came out before I could stop them. "The little girl. The picture in your wallet. Is that your daughter?"

His entire demeanour changed and he stopped. His shoulders fell, and the energy drained from his face. He nodded and opened his wallet to look at the picture in question.

"Her name's Akiko. She's only ten-years-old. She, uh, she went missing a few weeks ago." He blinked back tears. Another missing girl? This man's daughter, the man who called himself Yasu's fiancee, and Sayumi. Three women gone from the same town. That was no coincidence.

"Where did she go missing, if you don't mind my asking?"

The man shrugged, his eyes focused on the photo. "She was on her way home from school, I guess. She left as normal that day, but she never made it back. None of her friends saw her. No-one saw her. She was just… gone."

I didn't know what to say. "I'm sorry to hear that." An awkward silence filled the air. The clock ticked loudly above me. "The police don't know what happened?"

He shook his head. "They're searching for her, but they haven't found anything." He looked up at the roof and blinked a few times, then turned to me and forced a smile. "Anyway, thank you for this." He held the wallet up. "And thank you for the help yesterday. I hope…" He took a deep breath. "I hope that when Akiko gets back that we can enjoy them all together again."

The doorbell tinkled behind him and the store fell silent. Three girls missing without a trace. I rubbed my arms, the store colder than usual. What was going on?

As the day came to a close, I finished making notes of the day's sales in the store ledger and sighed. Sayumi's handwriting ended several pages earlier. After that, it was all me. Maths was never my strong point. The numbers all started to swirl together before long. I hated accounting and hoped Sayumi wouldn't find too many mistakes when she returned.

A storm raged outside. Wind picked up wet leaves and sent them tumbling through the air, punctuated by short bursts of light and the distant rumble of thunder. As a child I enjoyed storms. As an adult, they made me uneasy. Water conducted spirits and made it easier for them to come into our world.

A mother pulled her daughter close under their shared umbrella and I felt a twinge of jealousy. A young couple huddled under the man's jacket, giggling as they ran against the wind and water. It was dark outside, and soon the storefront would come to life; not with customers, but with something else. Something I didn't want to be around to see.

The young woman's photo stared back at me from the corner of the desk, a happy face that knew little struggle. I could see her past unravelling before me. She had a happy family and devoted partner. She probably played volleyball at school—captain of the team, no doubt—and aced all her tests. She went to a good university, met her now-fiance, and was living a happy life surrounded by happy people. The look on her face didn't know hardship or pain.

So, where was she now?

I reached out for the necklace, my fingers extending slowly as it came within reach. They hovered over it while my brain debated what would happen. Would it be like the little girl's photo? Or would it be like normal? Would I have to focus and let everything in while I looked for what I was after?

I withdrew my hand and closed my eyes. The antique clock above the register ticked. *Tick tock. Tick tock.* A rumble of thunder from far away filled the store, and it wouldn't be long before that wasn't the only thing.

"This sucks," I said to no-one in particular. How long did she expect me to carry on like this? Night after night of silence, of ignorance, of not knowing where she was, what she was doing, if she was hurt and when (or if) she might be back.

The street grew dark and empty. Most people

would be in the comfort of their homes by now, eating a hot dinner in a warm room, watching TV with their family and relaxing after a hard day's work. I closed the ledger and my eyes flickered back to the photo. Her family were missing her just as much as I was missing Sayumi, but worse. Sayumi told me she was leaving; a work trip, no less. But this girl, she disappeared without a word. Her family had no idea. I could help them. Whatever the risks, I could help them.

I picked up the piece of paper with the man's number and dialled. It rang a few times before a gruff "hello?" answered.

"Hello. This is Mako. From the Matsuda Tea and Sweets store."

Silence.

"…Hi."

"I'd like you to come back to the store again tomorrow. I'll take on your case. I'll help you find your fiancee."

5

"WHAT CAN YOU TELL ME about… what did you say her name was again?"

"Keiko," Yasu said. He shifted awkwardly from foot to foot. I put a tray of green tea down on the front counter and offered him some. "Thank you."

"Keiko," I repeated the word like it gave me power. Now I knew her. Her photo lay between us on the desk, happy face smiling up. "What does Keiko do?"

He warmed his hands around the cup and stilled his feet the best he could. "She works at a fashion boutique in the city. A sales clerk. Sells fancy, expensive clothes."

Yeah. Judging by the photo alone that fit her perfectly. I could hear her booming voice in my head every time a customer entered the store. "Welcome!" Her friendly manner. Laughing and slapping the customers on the shoulder at a poor joke, making them feel comfortable enough to shell out copious amounts of money for clothes she suggested to them. That seemed to suit her just fine.

"Okay. How long has she been working there?"

"She started part-time in university, and then when she graduated they took her on full-time. She works Monday to Friday, 8 to 4. Normal hours. She takes the train in, it's only three stops from our house so it's not too far, and leaves the house at 7:15 each morning. The train leaves at 7:23 exactly. She arrives at the station at 7:34 and from there it's a 10-minute walk to work."

I raised my eyebrows. "Well, that's… certainly very detailed. Thank you."

He nodded and took a sip of the tea. "This is good. Thank you."

I smiled. "We do specialise in tea, so I'm glad to hear it."

He looked around, seemingly taking in for the first time where he really was. "Uh, yes. Of course. How stupid of me."

I shook my head. "Okay, so on the day Keiko disappeared, you said she left for work as usual?"

He nodded. "There was nothing out of the ordinary. She got dressed, gave me a kiss on the cheek and left. I leave the house 10 minutes after her. She's usually on the train by that time. Around 10 a.m., I got a call from her boss. She wasn't at work and she didn't call in sick, so they wanted to know where she was. I told them she left as normal and called her phone, but there was no answer. It was like she just disappeared. We went to the police that evening, but they told us that this type of thing wasn't uncommon." Yasu scoffed at that.

"What did they mean by that? Not uncommon?"

"People go 'missing' all the time. They usually show up a few days later, safe and sound. Apparently the stress gets to be a little much sometimes and people take off, they said. But Keiko's not like that. She wasn't stressed. She had no reason to disappear like that. We have a happy life together, we do, and she enjoys her work. I just… I don't understand."

"I see." I took a sip of my own tea and stared at the photo.

"After she was gone a few days, the police finally agreed to put out a missing person's report for her. I called everyone we know, even old school friends we haven't seen in years." He put his cup down on the counter and leaned forward. "You don't understand. Keiko's… Keiko's parents are old. They're sick. We visit them each weekend. There's no way she would leave like this, not when they might…" His words trailed off and he bit his bottom lip. "Please. We're supposed to get married in a few weeks. Please. I don't know…" He fought back tears. "I don't know what I'm supposed to do without her."

The necklace sat atop the photo, a shining beacon screaming for me to touch it. To take it in my hands and open myself up to the other side. I reached out for it. Yasu was in the room. If anything happened… he might not be able to do much about it, but he could call an ambulance. Call the police. Whatever good that might do. I reached forward, closer, my fingertips just above the metal…

Ring ring. Ring ring.

I jumped and grabbed my chest, smiling apologetically at Yasu. “Sorry, I need to…” I picked up the phone, my heart hammering. “Hello? Matsuda Tea and Sweets.”

“Hello! This is Tanaka from Yoshien Tea Distributors. Is Ms Matsuda there by any chance?”

I turned away from Yasu. “Oh, um, no, she’s on vacation right now. She’ll be back shortly if you want to leave a message.”

I scribbled a note down and said goodbye to the man.

“Sorry about that.”

Yasu shook his head. He drained the rest of the tea and placed the cup back on the tray. “Can you help me?”

I looked at the photo. “Is there anything else? Anything else at all?”

Yasu shook his head. “What else do you need to know?”

That was a good question. “That should be enough. Thank you.” I replaced my cup on the tray and moved it aside.

“I’m going to do what I can to find your fiancée, Yasu, but I need you to know that I can’t guarantee anything, okay?”

Yasu nodded his head furiously, desperate for anything to help bring his fiancée back. “Yes, yes, of course.”

“I don’t know what I’ll find, if anything. It’s not an… exact process.” I’d never explained how I found things to people before. I never had to. Sayumi dealt with that side of the business. “But I’ll do what I can. I promise you that much.”

"Oh, thank you, thank you!" He reached out with his hands to shake mine, but I withdrew before he could touch me. He retracted his hands, confusion fleeting across his face. "Sorry, I…"

"No, no, it's okay." My cheeks blushed with embarrassment. "I don't want to mix things up. Just in case."

He didn't know what I was talking about, but he nodded a few times, anyway. "Okay, yeah, sure. I don't want to do anything that might mess with… whatever you do." He looked around the room, half-expecting pagan symbols to appear on the roof and floor, no doubt.

"If anything else comes up, I'll call you."

"Yeah, of course. Thank you." He took one last look at the photo and then bowed. "Seriously, thank you."

He exited with another bow at the door, then disappeared up the street. The girl's photo smiled up at me. I put my gloves on and hid it under the counter. There would be work to do later.

6

I TOOK THE PHOTO AND necklace upstairs after closing the store, to the safety of my room. After closing the door, I checked the window was shut tight and put the items down on the desk. I took off one glove, slowly, and then the other. This was it. I could do it. I didn't need Sayumi. The power was in me, after all. She'd trained me well and nothing was stopping me from doing this other than myself. Judgement time. I would not fail, and I wouldn't let anything drag me in. I had nothing to fear. It was just me, a photo, and the connection it led to. All I had to do was follow it. Simple. I sat down, focused on the necklace, and grasped it.

My vision swam. Images and colours swirled in and out. Up turned down, right turned left. Sounds reverberated in and out and I was outside of myself. Where was I? A forest? A body, swinging from a tree, feet dirty with mud. Another body, face down in the dirt, unmoving. The flashes hit me, one after another, and I struggled to keep up. A sign with *KUROHANA FOREST* in old, flaky letters. A young girl walking through the darkness, shadowy figures watching her unseen from the trees. Their heads turned in unison towards my direction.

They were looking right at me.

I screamed and dropped the necklace. The connection severed, but the sensations remained. I jumped out of the chair, brushing my arms and legs of invisible ants, invisible dirt, invisible eyes.

I glanced around the room. They saw me. They looked directly at me. They knew I was there, even though I wasn't, not really. The door was closed and the window shut. A chill filled the air, but there was no-one in the room but me. They didn't come back with me. I was safe. I was alone.

I was… alone.

Brushing my arms again, I sat down on the bed. The feelings wouldn't go away. Their eyes crawling all over me, invading me, finding me. Discovering me. Knowing me.

The woman, Keiko, was in a forest—Kurohana Forest—but she wasn't alone. A body swung from a tree, and yet another girl lay in the dirt. The images were familiar, like I'd been there before. I hadn't—not physically anyway—but I *had* been there. Just the day before when I picked up the photo of the little girl. It was the same place. The same colours, the same sensations, the same fear. Like the forest was alive, calling people to it and consuming them whole.

Branches scratched relentlessly at the window, an ungodly screech that reached into my chest and took hold, an iron grip that refused to let go. Something banged downstairs, and I jumped again. Just the house settling. That's all. The house was old, a part of Sayumi's family for generations. Old houses creaked and groaned all the time, especially during times of bad weather. It was nothing. Absolutely nothing. Besides, the things in the storefront never came upstairs. In the three years I'd been living there, nothing ever came upstairs. Nothing. They had their space, and I had my space. We respected each other and everything was fine.

I jumped. Another bang, this time closer. "Just the window," I said, hoping the sound of my voice would make me feel a little less alone. It had the opposite effect; I was more keenly aware than ever that it was just me in a big old house at the end of a desolate street, the remains of yet another rainy, windy day lashing the trees outside. It was just the wind. Just the house settling. Just…

"Ah!"

I scooted back across the bed, pressing myself into the corner. The door handle jiggled. That wasn't the wind. Sayumi's door was Japanese-style; a gorgeous sliding door decorated with various flowers. When it was windy, it often clattered and banged on its frame. That was normal. My door was Western. It had a metal handle and lock and it took force to move.

No. I shook my head. They couldn't have followed me back. Not that quickly. It was just a second. I let go before they found me. I let go before they infected me. They couldn't have…

Jiggle jiggle.

"Go away!"

I pulled the blanket up closer, a protective barrier between myself and whatever was on the other side of the door. Wiry stick fingers scratched at the window, motioning for me to come outside. There's no-one here to help you now. It's futile. Come. Join us.

"Salt..." Of course. I dove for the desk and yanked the bottom drawer open. Several boxes of table salt stared back at me. I fumbled, my fingers cold and not listening to my commands. I tore the top off the box and ran to the door. Salt spilt all over the floor and I dumped the rest in two piles on either side.

"You're not welcome here!" The wind picked up outside and the scratching on the window continued. Something else creaked downstairs. I waited. My heart thumped in my chest and it was like time slowed down. *Badump. Badump. Badump.* The salt sizzled. My eyes burned a hole into the door. *Badump. Badump.* The top of the salt piles turned black. The window creaked. *Badump. Badump.*

The salt fell silent. It stop fizzing and the charred top settled. The door handle was still and the house calm. It was gone. I was alone.

Alone.

Leaving the lights on, I crawled under the blankets. I screwed up. I knew I shouldn't have attempted to find something without Sayumi's guidance. She was the one who helped me along, who pointed me in the right direction and kept me from harm. I wasn't ready to do this without her.

I had invited something into her house and she wasn't here to help me.

I was alone.

All alone...

7

"HELLO? MATSUDA TEA AND SWEETS."

"Hello. This is Mrs Tamita."

My breath caught in my throat as I picked up the phone the next morning. Mrs Tamita. Another customer who didn't come to the store for tea but for the… side business.

"Mrs Tamita. Good morning! How are you feeling today?"

"Oh, you know. The same as usual. My hip is popping and cracking, and it's a struggle to get up in the morning, but at my age, well, what else can you expect?" She laughed, the epitome of a sweet little old lady, but there was a sadness behind it as well. "I don't suppose you've had any luck with the item I requested?"

My heart sank as I remembered the previous night's events. Mrs Tamita was looking for a family photo album, a job Sayumi accepted a month earlier. The family moved houses, and it wasn't until a few weeks in their new abode that they realised they couldn't find the album. They must have left it in the old house, but when they went back to find it, it was nowhere to be seen. All that remained was a single photo of it. Mrs Tamita and her late husband were in the foreground, their children playing on the floor behind them, and the album was sitting on a bookshelf in the background. So much was happening in the photo that I had been struggling to pin the album down. My attempts pulled me back and forth, giving me images of Mrs Tamita herself, the children in the photo, and even her deceased husband. Finding a person wasn't very difficult. The connection between a person and one of their possessions was strong, but finding an item was another matter altogether.

"I, uh, no, not yet. Ms Matsuda is on vacation right now, but we'll find your album. I promise." I wasn't sure I could keep that promise, but the old lady seemed happy to hear it, regardless.

"Oh good, good. That album holds some of my most precious memories of my husband, you know." I did. "I just…" Her voice trailed off and my heart dropped. "I just want to see them again."

"I understand, Mrs Tamita. We'll do our best, don't worry. You'll get your album back. We're still looking. It's being a little difficult, but you know what Ms Matsuda always says; hardship shapes character… or something like that."

"If you do find anything, you will let me know, won't you?"

"Of course, Mrs Tamita. Don't worry. It's not over yet. We'll find your album."

"Thank you, my dear. You don't know how much that thing means to an old woman like me." Sadness filled her voice again.

"We'll find it soon. I assure you."

I hung up the phone and rubbed my temples. The album. I entirely forgot about the album. The photo sat in my desk upstairs, untouched after Sayumi left. Mrs Tamita was ill and didn't have much time left, and all she wanted was that photo album back. The last link to her memories of her husband. The store was empty. I pursed my lips and flipped the sign on the front of the store to CLOSED and went upstairs. The piles of salt sat blackened by the door. I walked through them and removed the photo from the desk.

"Why me?" I sighed.

In my experiences "finding" things with Sayumi, there was always a certain degree of danger, but it varied. Inanimate objects were harder to find, but safer. There was, in general, no energy attached to those. Nothing negative that could follow me home, or attempt to drag me in. People—living creatures—were another matter entirely. Easy to find, near-immediate in most cases, and as the little girl's photo the other day reminded me, sometimes without any effort on my part whatsoever.

Too many people and objects clouded the photo. Narrowing just the album down was proving difficult, and after the previous night's events, I didn't exactly want to jump straight in again. But Mrs Tamita was old. The album was one of the last remaining things of her late husband. She might not have much more time left. I turned to the salt pile. My heart hammered in my chest. Bile rose in my throat and the jiggling of the door handle echoed inside my head. Did I really want to do this again? And so soon? Items were safer, I reminded myself. I'd searched the photos several times with no result on any front.

Succumb to my fear. Help a dying old woman with her final request.

What choice did I have?

"Screw it. Here goes nothing."

I gripped the edges of the photo and focused. For a moment I saw nothing, and then colours and lines spread out before me. Visions and sensations jumbled into a rainbow of sensory overload. A needle in a haystack. I could dig through the hay for hours and never find what I was looking for, but if I spent long enough in there, something else might find me. That was how it worked.

Mrs Tamita was sitting on her couch, sobbing. A young woman, presumably her now-grown up granddaughter, was taking a test. Anxiety and nausea filled me, spreading throughout me like a wave. An important test. A life-ending test. Sobs. Fear. Nerves. A young man playing soccer. Adrenaline. Exhaustion. Jubilation.

Focus, Mako. Focus. People always stand out the brightest. Ignore them. Look around them. They're not what you want. The album. Focus on the album. It's out there somewhere. You can do this. When Sayumi returns, you'll tell her that you found it. Your first successful job all alone.

Alone.

Fear flooded my veins. Invisible eyes on the soccer field turned my way. The sky darkened. The hair on the back of my neck stood on end. My neck? Or someone else's? My chest rose and fell, rose and fell, increasing in speed. Hyperventilating. I couldn't breathe. No, not me. Cries. It hurt so much. So, so much. Why did he leave me? Being alone hurt so much. Why did they always leave me? A delivery truck. Darkness. Stuffiness. Hard to breathe. The corner. In the. Corner.

The album!

No, not a truck. Not anymore. The album. Follow it. Eyes were on me, increasing in number. Getting closer. I was a lighthouse and they were lost at sea. They would keep coming in increasing numbers. Closer.

Rubbish. Rubbish everywhere. Cold. So cold. The album, yes, there it was. Its unique signature, faint, but it swirled and answered my call. It was in the rubbish, thrown out by cleaners too lazy to find its rightful owner.

The eyes. They swam closer, no longer adrift but with purpose. The darkness. It expanded. It called. It drove with purpose. They were coming. Once again they were coming. The album was right there. I recognised its signature. It was weak, but it was there.

A biting cold drifted over my arm. Goosebumps rose on my skin. Another tendril snaked around my leg. No. I was so close. I needed more time. A flick of cold on the back of my neck.

"No!" I let go of the photo. The salt piles remained stationary. No fizzing, no hissing, no blackening. The room was just as I left it. They were close, too close, but I had picked up the signature of the album, and without Sayumi's assistance. I had done it.

So why was I still covered in goosebumps?

8

I'M TELLING YOU GUYS, KUROHANA Forest is haunted. Like, the trees are alive or something, seriously. I used to pass by on my way to school, and even from the train you can, like, feel it calling to you or something. It's a popular suicide spot. Everyone knows that. People only go into that forest when they never plan on coming back out again, you know? The trees are so thick and dense that if you wander off the track, you'll never find your way back out again. It all looks the same. You'll walk in circles for hours, no idea where you are, and then…

The text continued. It was just after closing time and the house was eerily quiet. I scrolled down the page on my phone, but it was more of the same. Kurohana Forest. I knew of it, but not well. It was a half hour drive away, and I'd never been there personally, but the name wasn't foreign to me either. I'd heard stories. The stories were enough to kill any ideas I might have about hiking there.

All the searches said the same thing. Suicide spot. Haunted forest. Don't go in. It's dangerous. Once you go in, you'll never come back out. You'll be cursed. The ghosts will make you one of them. On and on it went. Kurohana Forest was a bad place you didn't want to be in. It was also the location of at least two missing girls that had come to my attention.

What was going on?

Keiko's necklace lay discarded where I dropped it the night before. Its connection to Keiko was so strong that it instantly drew me in, and it wanted me to know where she was. Well, not technically 'it.' Keiko did. Her energy. Whatever it was. Kurohana Forest. I'm in Kurohana Forest. Come and find me. Please.

I put my gloves on and picked up the necklace, placing it in a small bag with the photo. That would solve any unwanted touching for the time being, but it was clear what my next move had to be. Keiko was in Kurohana. I had to go there.

I typed a new search into the computer. A private train line stopped just a five-minute walk from the forest. What to do? I was the only person running the store; I couldn't just pop on over to the forest for a few minutes, drag Keiko out, and then everything would be over. It needed planning, preparation, and the right state of mind. It also needed to be after work, and my heart sank. After work meant darkness. A dark forest in the cold of night. Well, how much worse could it be than a dark house in the cold of night? At least I knew there were people in the forest… alive or otherwise.

After work, then, when everything was ready. I would take the train over, assess the situation, and with enough lighting, protection, and a way to make sure I could find my way out safely, everything would be fine.

"Think things through carefully." Sayumi's voice echoed in my head. "Don't go into matters half-cocked. That's when mistakes happen, and you of all people can't afford mistakes. You need to be thorough, but most of all, you need to be safe. If you misjudge a situation, it's life or death, literally. You're different, Mako. Special. You're half in, half out, for better or for worse. You need to be more careful than other people, and you need to be smarter, too. Take your time. Get things right the first time because there may not be a second."

She never explained what she meant by "half in, half out." I had my suspicions, but I never brought them up. Kurohana Forest needed detailed plans. I would be safe and I would be certain. My first field mission all by myself. I'd show Sayumi I could do it. She wouldn't always be around. It was about time I started taking care of myself. Learn how to stand on my own two legs.

A soft buzz and the sound of voices filtered upstairs. The TV? I could have sworn I turned it off. I got up and walked past Sayumi's door, stopping to do a double take. A figure was standing over her bed. A darkness in the dim light looking down at the empty space where she usually slept. It turned to look at me, but when I turned back, it was gone. I shook my head. No, I was just seeing things. I was tired. It had been a rough few weeks, and the last few days especially had me run off my feet. Exhaustion played tricks on the mind, and for someone like me, that meant seeing things that may or may not exist. The house was clean and free of ghosts; the second floor was, anyway. Talismans and charms decorated the walls to ward off evil. That part of the business was also in Sayumi's family for generations, or so she said.

This whole Kurohana business and the photo album and running the store alone was getting to me. I wasn't sleeping well. Once I saw the forest for myself, got the album back for the old woman, and once I cleared my head, then everything would be back to normal. Or, mostly normal. Who knew, Sayumi might come back the next morning, her job successfully completed and I wouldn't have to worry about it anymore. I could sleep soundly again and we'd laugh at how scared I was, worried that she'd gone missing after only a few short weeks. It wasn't the first time, so why was I acting like a puppy without its owner? The photo on Sayumi's desk smiled back at me. That's right. I'm an adult. The dark doesn't scare me. I know what's in the dark; I've seen it with my own two eyes, many times.

The house creaked, and I jumped. "Now you're just playing with me." The words seemed to echo off the walls, highlighting how empty the house was with only me in it.

I hurried downstairs to turn the rogue TV off.

9

A KNOCK AT THE DOOR caught my attention. My heart dropped. Hiroshi, the delivery guy. He pointed at a few boxes on the ground and grinned. I wasn't in the mood to deal with him again.

"I thought you were going to keep me waiting out there forever!" he said as I opened the door. "Phew, sure is cold out there, don't you think?"

"I'm used to the cold."

"Yeah, sure, no, it's nothing. Anyway, another delivery for the lovely Matsuda Tea and Sweets, if you could just sign here."

I took the pen and scribbled my name. "Thank you." He dropped the boxes off and, as I suspected he would, followed me back to the front counter.

"So, I see Ms Matsuda is still on vacation, huh?"

"You were only here a few days ago, so yes, she's still on vacation." It was difficult to keep the venom out of my words. Something about him rubbed me the wrong way. Why was it so difficult for him to just do his job and leave? Why did he constantly have to pry? It was unbecoming.

"Sure, sure, yeah. Just making conversation."

I grabbed one of the boxes and started cutting it open. Maybe that would give him a clue to leave, but instead he leaned on the counter and watched me.

"You know, it's not really safe for a beautiful young lady such as yourself to be working here all alone."

My skin crawled. "I'm fine, thank you. I'm sure you have a lot of deliveries to get back to."

"I mean, you're all the way out here, basically the middle of nowhere with little traffic other than what comes to the store. Even if you screamed for help, who would come running?"

Alarm bells rang. I tore open the tabs of the cardboard box and forced my lips shut.

"Why didn't you call me the other day? I left my number. It was the correct number, right? Where's your phone, I can put my number in there for you, just to make sure."

I stood up and slammed my hands on the box. "Sir, I think it would be best for you to go now." I couldn't take it anymore. He was either extremely ignorant or extremely rude, but the end result was the same. It had to stop.

He put his hands up in the air and took a step back. "Hey, calm down." He laughed. "I'm just trying to be friendly. You seem lonely here, that's all. I thought you might be shy. Sometimes you've gotta take the initiative or things will never happen, you know? Look, why don't we have lunch together, my treat. My way of saying sorry. I'm sorry if I came across as a little pushy, I just... there's a nice ramen store on the corner up there, right? I'm sure you've been there many times before. Why don't we go there together?"

I clenched my fists until my knuckles turned white. "Hiroshi, yes?"

He beamed. "That's right."

"Thank you for the delivery. You should go."

He nodded and took a few steps back. "Yeah, sure, my bad. I overstepped my boundaries, okay. I was just trying to be friendly. I mean, you're all alone out here in the middle of nowhere, you know? You seemed sad. I can see it in your eyes. You want a friend. Someone to protect you, is my guess."

The filth spewing from his mouth brought the contents of my stomach back up, and I wondered if he knew how he sounded to the outside world.

"There's not much traffic out this way. Every time I've come here the store has been empty, you know? Well, anyway, my bad. I was just trying to help." He grabbed the door handle. "I wonder how long this place can stay in business without many people around. I was going to help, but—"

"Please go." It took all I had not to throw the box at him. He smiled.

"I'll see you next time."

My hands shook; whether in fear or anger, I couldn't tell. He got back in the truck, gave a friendly wave, and drove off up the street. At least part of what he said was true; the shop wasn't getting a lot of traffic lately, and without Sayumi around to brighten things up, fewer and fewer customers were buying.

The storefront seemed to darken. I put my jacket on and kept the phone nearby; just in case.

I retreated to the back room after work. It was a combined break/lounge room with a tiny kitchen in the back and a TV and couch on the other side. I didn't watch much TV, but after the day I had, some background noise seemed like just the thing. I was reminded of the TV turning itself on the night before. Between that and the lights constantly flickering on and off in the storefront, it was clear that something was wonky with the house wiring, but I wasn't sure if I should call an electrician in Sayumi's stead. I flicked through the channels until I came across a pair of entertainers making their way through Africa. They were attempting to communicate, unsuccessfully, with a local tribe. It was better than nothing. I let it play and grabbed a book from the shelf.

Zhoomp.

"What the hell?"

The room went black. I pressed the POWER button on the remote over and over, but nothing. I flicked the light switch and no response. My heart raced. Maybe waiting for Sayumi's return wasn't the best course of action.

"The breaker?" I wondered.

No need to panic. This sort of thing happened all the time in old places. It was fine. The breaker was by the back door, all I had to do was go down the hallway and flick it back on. I put a hand on the wall and fumbled my way to the other end of the house. It was dark and silent, but no spirits were waiting to jump out and grab me. No intruder waiting to stab me and rob the store blind. Nothing but an old house unable to handle an increase of power for the moment. That was it. An electrician could fix it later. I reached up and flicked the switch. The TV roared to life in the other room. See. Nothing to worry about.

I returned to the break room and sat down. I reached for the book again and *zhoomp*. Darkness. Twice in a row wasn't the breaker. Adrenaline pushed me out of the chair and I pressed my ear against the door. Too quiet. A door slammed suddenly and I jumped.

It was him. The delivery guy. Hiroshi. It had to be. It was too obvious, but it was so obvious that it looped back around to him again. He was behind it. I hurt his feelings by ignoring his advances and now he was carrying out exactly what he said would happen. He was proving a point.

"Shit!"

I reached for the phone and grabbed air. I was using it earlier in the store and must have left it there. Dammit.

"Think, Mako. Think."

The only way to get to the safety of my room was down the hall and back up the stairs. If he was already at the back door, that option was out. Only the storefront remained, and the phone was there as well, but it was dark. Darkness was *their* domain, not ours. It was an unspoken agreement. They stayed in the front and we stayed upstairs. We each had our personal space and didn't intrude upon the other. I jumped at another bang, this time closer.

The front was my only option unless I wanted to face the intruder head-on. For a brief moment that almost seemed preferable.

I pushed the door open with a creak and stuck my head around the corner. The hall was pitch black. To the left was the back door and stairs; to the right the door leading to the front. After confirming nobody was in the hall, I tip-toed to the right and slipped through. I got to my hands and knees and closed my eyes. 'I'm sorry,' I apologised in my head. 'This is your space, I know. I'll be out of your hair as soon as possible. I'm sorry.'

Crawling towards the front counter, I fumbled for the phone. It fell and I caught it in my lap. Safe. I put it to my ear, but it beeped like it was already in use. I hung up, over and over, and pressed 110 for the police, but nothing. Somebody was blocking the line.

Hiroshi.

I closed my eyes, kept my head down, and crawled back towards the door. The hair on the back of my neck stood on end and chills ran down my arms and legs. They were close.

'I'm sorry, I'm sorry.'

I reached up and grabbed the door handle; it was ice cold. A wisp of cold air brushed past my ankle and I jumped through the open door. I leaned back against it, my breath coming in ragged. It was only a few seconds, but they moved on me in an instant.

I could still feel their cold tendrils running over my skin as they brushed past. Who were they? What did they want? Ugh. It didn't matter, there was still the tiny matter of the intruder in the house to attend to. The phone was no good. Perhaps the bathroom? I could hide in there for a while and wait it out. No, hiding wouldn't do any good. I needed help. If I could slip out the back, I could run up the street and get help. The street was full of pure businesses, unlike Sayumi's combined home, but there had to be someone nearby. There had to be. Anything that didn't require me going through the front…

I pressed myself against the wall and took careful, methodical steps. With each step I confirmed that I was alone, and that nothing was nearby. Where was he? Still in the house? Or was he playing cat and mouse for fun? I inched down the hall, step by step, listening and waiting. The house was silent. Almost too silent, considering the usual moans and groans it made as night fell. I reached the back door and grabbed the handle. I jiggled it a few times and pushed. Stuck. He had jammed the door closed. Did that mean he was inside or out?

It didn't matter. The only way out was through the front unless I went upstairs and climbed out my second-floor window. I had no veranda; it was a straight drop to the ground below. The considerable drop was not a deterrent compared to the only other option available. Go upstairs, open the window, jump out. I wouldn't have to go out through the front, but the chances of spraining something were high. If that happened, however, and he was outside, it was all over. And if he was inside… it was probably still all over.

The front was a straight line. Down the hall, through the door, and then a few metres to the entrance. It was the clearest and simplest route. I could run and be out of the house in just a few short seconds. All I had to do was go through *them*.

I didn't know who they were, and the one time I asked Sayumi about the strange presence I felt in the storefront after dark, she said, "We don't go there at night." That was it. She smiled and patted my shoulder and walked away like that explained everything. "We don't go there at night." I had no other choice.

I crouched down and ran towards the door. Reaching up for the handle, I took a deep breath and steadied myself. Just a few short metres away, freedom awaited. You can do this. Don't disturb them, don't look at them, don't acknowledge them. Just go for the door and get out.

I pushed and crawled across the floor as fast as I could. My shoulder hit a shelf and bags of tea tumbled to the ground. I ignored them and kept going. Eyes fell upon me instantly. I was in their territory, disturbing their peace. I slid across the cool floor and hit another shelf. Everything was dark; if I opened my eyes, I would see them. I couldn't allow that to happen. They closed in. The air grew heavy and cold, pushing in on me, sucking out the oxygen I had stored in my lungs. Something called out to me, an incorporeal voice that knew my name. "Mako~" I shook my head. Cold tendrils drifted across my ankle and up my calf. They snaked across my shoulder. They brushed across my hair.

I hit something hard and reached up. The front door. The handle, just grab the handle…

Something screamed upstairs, an ear-piercing scream that shattered the night silence. I opened my eyes and saw them. Countless figures in the dark, crowding around me, pushing in on me. They turned in unison to the sound upstairs. I pushed back against the door, willing myself to melt through the glass and end up on the other side. Footsteps thudded on the stairs and something crashed like a door being thrust open. Then… silence.

I ran. I threw the door to the hall open and ran all the way to the back. The lock lay on the ground, and the door swung back and forth in the breeze. A chair lay on its side in the wet grass, but the yard was empty. I pulled the door closed—the best I could with the handle busted—and made my way upstairs. The stairs creaked beneath my feet, mingling with the pounding of my heart in my eardrums. I hurried past Sayumi's dark room and found my door wide open. Blood covered the pen on my desk, and a few drops stained the wooden floor below. The drawers sat open and various items were strewn around the room, but it was otherwise empty. The intruder was gone.

What on earth had happened?

10

"WELCOME!" A LARGE VOICE BOOMED as I stepped into the ramen shop for lunch. A waitress I had a passing familiarity with greeted me and guided me in. "Would you prefer a table or counter seat?"

"Counter," I said. The events of the previous night had shaken me and I wanted to be near people. Not necessarily to talk to them, just to be in their presence. Safety in numbers. I figured that listening to other people as background noise would be a nice reminder that I wasn't alone.

The waitress cleared away a few empty bowls and I sat down. "Let me know when you're ready to order." I visited the ramen shop on occasion, but not enough to remember the waitress's name. Her name tag said *AKARI* in large letters. Her name was Akari. Somehow knowing that made me feel better, like we were less estranged. Now I knew something personal about her, and that was the first step in eliminating the unknown. It was in the unknown that fear lay. I was done with fear.

"I'll have a regular miso ramen, please," I answered.

"Certainly," Akari smiled. She wrote a memo and slapped it on the board for the chef out back to see. "Anything else?" She put a cup of hot tea down before me. I shook my head. "Okay. We'll bring your meal when it's ready."

I nodded and took a sip. An unfortunate side effect of working in a tea store with a boss who was obsessed with the different qualities and tastes of tea was that I unconsciously judged everything I received. It was a mild blend of bancha; a personal favourite of mine. A little cheap, but not unexpected of a restaurant such as this, and it was pleasant nonetheless. I warmed my hands around the mug and took in the conversations taking place around me.

"I wanna buy a house in the city."

"We've discussed this. I'm not making enough at work right now to afford that. What's wrong with Shirotama? Both our families are here, so we don't have to travel far for special occasions, and the cost of living is cheap."

"But it's so boring here. We've been here all our lives. I want to go somewhere new."

"That's why holidays exist."

A young couple were arguing over their future. It was pleasant; neither was accusing the other nor raising their voice. They slurped their ramen between answers and, although the woman huffed and puffed, she looked at her partner with complete devotion. I smiled despite myself. How nice to find someone who would look at you like that without even realising it.

"Mama! Mama! I wanna go to a big park for my birthday! A big one!" A small boy, perhaps only seven-years-old, was bouncing in his seat next to his mother.

"You'll have to ask your father, dear."

The boy turned expectantly to him. "Papa! Papa! Can we go?"

The father slurped his ramen without looking up. "Ask your mother."

"Mama! Mama!"

Next to them, two police officers were having lunch, one engrossed in his noodles while the other was engrossed in his newspaper.

"You know they're talking about budget cuts again, right?"

The officer eating his noodles nodded his head and slurped a particularly long noodle. "They talk about it every year. If they went through on everything they said, we'd all be living in mansions and homeless at the same time. They're fools."

"I can't afford to take a wage cut." The officer turned the page of his newspaper. "I'm struggling enough it is, and now Ayumi's threatening to leave me."

His partner laughed out loud, drawing the eyes of a few customers in the store. "Sorry. But can you blame her? You're never there! I'm surprised she hasn't left your sorry ass already."

The other officer closed his paper and looked up. "I'm never there because I'm always working to provide for her!"

His partner held his hands in the air and nodded. "Sure, sure, I'm not judging. I'm not the one telling you to spend all your time and hard-earned money in the snack bar each night."

"I don't..." The man sighed and smacked his partner over the head with the rolled up newspaper. "It's not like that. It's just to unwind after a hard day working with an ass like you."

"Sure, sure. But what really gets me is the constant stream of cases they've been piling on our desks lately. Like, I get that we're understaffed, but it seems that every day we get a new case, and it's almost always someone missing."

My ears perked up.

"Yeah. This is supposed to be the quiet time of year, and I'm not getting home till after midnight most nights. Do you know how cold it is then?"

"Do you? Doesn't all that booze warm you up?"

"Shut up. But if I have to knock on one more door and ask 'Have you seen this girl?' I'm gonna go nuts."

"Are you okay?"

The waitress's concerned voice drew me back from the conversation.

"I'm sorry?"

She smiled and put the bowl of ramen down before me. "Sorry if it's none of my business, you just looked a little sad, is all."

"Oh!" I smiled and shook my head. "No, no. Well, not really. Kind of. I suppose."

The waitress—Akari, as her name tag reminded me—smiled.

"My mentor... my boss... Technically she's

both… she's on holidays, but I haven't heard from her since she left." I tasted the soup broth and warmth spread throughout my chest. "And someone broke into our house last night while she was gone."

Akari poured herself a cup of tea and took a sip. "What? I don't know what you can do about that first one, but if someone broke into your house, you really should report it to the police."

I turned to look at the two officers sitting in the corner. The one with the newspaper was hitting his laughing buddy again with it.

"I don't want to bother them."

Akari laughed. "That's kind of their job."

"I know, but… well I don't have any proof, and nothing was taken, so…"

Akari nodded. She leaned forward and lowered her voice. "To be honest, I don't think the cops in this town are the greatest, anyway. Just last week there was some guy in here hassling me on his lunch break, right, asking me to go out with him and pestering me for my number. I told him to leave, and he got all upset. He was a paying customer, he said, and I ought to show him some respect. He got all loud and violent, so much that the boss had to come and kick him out himself."

Hiroshi flashed through my mind.

"We told the police about what happened and, of course, they were like, there's nothing we can do, he didn't commit any crime. Well, sure, but he sure did cause a fuss, and the boss has had to walk me home ever since because that very same day he was outside waiting for me."

"No way. Can't you get a restraining order

against him?" I asked. Akari shook her head.

"We tried. They said there's no evidence of stalking, and happening to be in the same place at the same time wasn't a crime. He hasn't done anything wrong yet, and they can't arrest him until he does. Stupid, right? I have to wait for him to kidnap and murder me before they'll do anything... Lotta good it'll do by then."

I bit into a piece of pork and let the sounds wash over me for a moment. Not even a busy ramen restaurant was safe, huh?

"I think the person who broke in last night... I don't have proof, mind you, but... a few days ago a delivery driver came to our store and he started acting the same way. Asking me out and pestering me for my number. He did it several times and never really took the hint to go away."

Akari straightened up. "Was he about this tall?" She held her hands about a head-length above her own. "Kinda shaggy black hair and thin?"

I swallowed and my eyes widened. That was enough of a response for Akari. "No way. It's gotta be the same guy."

"Hiroshi," I said. "His name is Hiroshi. I've seen him a few times before, but he always dealt with Sayumi... I mean my boss."

Akari shook her head, getting angrier by the second. "That scum... we really should report him, if not to the police then to his company or something."

As nice as that sounded, what the police said was true. Until he actually did something, there was nothing either of us could do. Being a creep wasn't a crime, and despite my suspicions, I had no proof that he was the one who broke into our house.

"You should be careful," Akari said. She scribbled down a number on a piece of paper and gave it to me. "My number, in case he ever drops by when you're alone again. You work at Matsuda Tea and Sweets, right?"

I tilted my head. "How did you know?"

"Well, there's only one tea shop in town, so…" She smiled.

Of course. "Thank you. I… I will." I put the piece of paper in my bag. I barely knew this woman any better than Hiroshi the Delivery Guy, but having a friend in this whole confused and messed up situation made me feel better, regardless.

"Seriously, if anything happens, give me a call. Me and the boss can come running down to save you." She laughed, throwing a fake punch. "We girls gotta look out for each other."

I smiled. I had few friends outside of Sayumi. "We do. Thank you."

"I'm worried that one of these days he's gonna go a little too far, you know? Like, actually kidnap a girl or something."

Kidnap a girl… there was far too much of that going on. But how was I, one lonely woman working in a little tea shop on the edge of town, supposed to do that?

11

I JUMPED ON THE TRAIN after work. It was a small, private line, and the train was only two cars long. Darkness settled over the area and I, along with two others, sat in the quiet, dim car as it chugged along. The swinging and swaying tempted me to sleep, lulling me into a false sense of relaxation. An old light crackled and fizzed above me while the old lady to my left nodded off. To my right, a businessman sat reading his newspaper.

The trip to Kurohana Station wasn't far, but as the train rocked, I felt the lure of sleep almost too difficult to fight, like the train didn't want me to be awake as we passed. *It would be better if you slept*, it was trying to tell me. *You don't want to go there.*

The old woman got off two stations later, leaving myself and the businessman. He folded up his paper, crossed his arms, and rested his head on his chest. The light buzzed and flashed a few times. The sun was long gone, and while the train was warm, I could sense the chill settling in outside. I didn't want to go out there. I wanted to be at home, safe in bed with my warm blanket and perhaps a good book. Even a bad book would do. Anything that wasn't me, here, attempting to go into a cursed forest at night. Although home didn't feel safe now either…

As if on cue, the train pulled up to Kurohana Station. I stepped outside into the cold night air and barely had enough time to look at the station sign before the train took off again. It swayed left and right, left and right. *You shouldn't have gotten off there. I tried to tell you. You're on your own now.*

I pulled my jacket closer. Kurohana Station had no attendant, and like the little train chugging away, there was a single overhead light that crackled and buzzed. *You don't want to be here either. Get out, go, while you still can!*

Kurohana Forest was visible from the station, only a few minutes' walk away. The sign from my vision rose lonely in front of it, dirty and rotting away, the characters barely legible. The forest was, back in the day, a popular spot with locals and tourists alike. Then it fell into decline and few people visited anymore. The only people who went in were those who didn't plan to come back out.

Pulling a roll of string out of my pocket, I walked towards the forest. I had every intention of returning, and hopefully in one piece as well. I didn't know what tricks the forest had up its sleeve, but I didn't intend on becoming another of its victims. This was a simple reconnaissance mission. Have a look around, see what I could find, and perhaps discover whether Keiko (or the little girl) were really there. It couldn't be a coincidence.

"Alright." I took a deep breath, held it for a moment, then exhaled. My breath, visible in the cold air, dissipated before me. I tied the string around a tree, pulled out my torch, and set it to the strongest beam. "Let's go."

A small dirt path led into the trees, wide enough for three or four people to walk side by side. Yet as I followed it deeper into the forest, it grew smaller. Soon, only two people could stand side by side, and then finally, one.

There was nothing out of the ordinary. I shone the light at my feet, then up and around the trees. I shone it high into their branches, hoping against hope that I didn't see anything up there. The dirt path disappeared, and before long I had to continue through the trees without direction. I unspooled the thread as I walked. It wouldn't last forever, but it should last long enough to give me a better idea of what I was facing.

"Hello?" I called out. I cringed at how loud my voice sounded in the darkness. "Is anyone there?"

Was no answer better than the alternative? Leaves and branches crunched beneath my feet, but there was no reply, ghostly or otherwise, to my call. Trees closed in around me, and as I spun my torch around, I realised just how similar they looked. No wonder they said it was so easy to get lost in here. There was nothing to distinguish where I was. The trees all looked the same; the same size, the same width, even their branches looked like they agreed to grow at the same points at the same time so as not to stand out.

"Hello?"

Not even an insect chirped or cried.

"What am I even looking for?"

There were no bodies hanging from trees. No bodies lying in the dirt. No chimes ringing in the distance. Just a sea of trees that spread out in all directions, nothing to distinguish one from the next. I tugged on the string again, just to be sure. It pulled taut. Relief spread throughout my veins.

"Sayumi?" I didn't know why I called out for her; if she was there in the first place, surely she would have responded to my initial call. But I wanted to check. I wanted to be sure.

"Don't look for me."

How could I not? Two weeks without word, and each passing day my fear that the worst had come to pass grew. She was on a job so dangerous that she felt the need to leave me out of it entirely; a job so dangerous that if things went wrong, she didn't want me to follow her for fear that I would get dragged into it as well. She had to know that I couldn't just leave it be. Sayumi was the only family I had left. Not blood family, of course, but that didn't matter.

Like myself, Sayumi lost both her parents when she was a child. She went to live with her grandparents in the Matsuda Tea and Sweets store and, when she got older, made it her personal mission to help out children whenever she could, particularly young girls struggling with family problems like she did. That was how she found me. That was why I couldn't just sit back and wait for her while she was potentially in trouble somewhere. If she needed help, then I had to find her.

"Don't look for me."

I shook my head. "Sayumi!" I called out again. The forest shuddered in reply.

12

LEAVES CRUNCHED BENEATH MY FEET. Twigs snapped and pebbles pressed into my shoes. As I walked, the trees grew so dense that even the moonlight found it difficult to penetrate their upper branches. I tugged on the thread and it pulled tight. Still good. I'd be able to follow it back to the start if needs be.

It was impossible to tell if anyone had been in the area recently. There were no tracks, and I was no hunter. I couldn't read the telltale signs a professional might. There were no footprints, nor could I tell if a stick was freshly broken by someone treading on it or if it had been that way for years. I couldn't even tell my own tracks behind me, and if it weren't for the string, I had no doubt that I would be completely and utterly lost. This was why people said that those who entered never returned. If you wanted to disappear and never be seen again, this would be a great place to do it.

I continued further in. The end of the string was in sight; a little further and it would run out entirely. Then I would be faced with a difficult decision: continue further without it (just a little…) or give up and go back. There was no sign of the missing girls, nor any evidence that Sayumi had been through either. That didn't mean much; it was a big forest, a veritable sea of trees that covered more ground than my little piece of string could hope to cover in a single night. But there was only one entrance, and it made sense that anyone entering would come through the same path. After that, however…

"Hello?"

Still nothing but darkness and the chill settling into my bones. As I walked, however, the forest seemed to grow unnaturally quiet. The leaves and sticks beneath my feet snapped loudly like an echo chamber. Somewhere eyes were upon me. I shone my torch around, spinning in a circle. They were out there; their gazes piercing me as plain as day. My heart beat faster, but I saw nothing.

"I know you're out there!"

I didn't know anything, but on the off chance that someone *was* watching me, and I hoped against hope that it was a someone and not a something, I didn't want them to know that.

"Please, I'm here to help!"

If they wanted help, they made no attempt at letting me know. Keiko's necklace throbbed in my pocket. If she was nearby, the pull would be stronger. All I had to do was take off my gloves, reach in, and grab it. The necklace was a direct link to her. If Keiko was nearby, it would lead me right to her. But it would also link me to *them*.

"Hello? I don't mean you any harm!" I couldn't say the same for whatever was watching me. I spun the torch around, but I didn't expect to see anything. The necklace in my pocket called to me, but I resisted it. It was a last resort, and if I could avoid opening myself up to the spirits of the forest, I would. I had no desire to become the newest of their numbers.

As I walked in silence, I noticed something else. Footsteps. Faint, but somewhere in the distance, slightly out of step with my own. There was no denying it. They were footsteps. Crunching on the dry leaves just beyond sight.

"Hello? Is anyone out there?"

Still no response.

"Are you hurt?"

Nothing. I started walking and the footsteps picked up again, almost in unison with my own. They weren't lost. They were following me. I picked up the pace, pushing myself through the dense trees. The string caught on a branch and I hurried to unravel it, my fingers fumbling with the delicate wool. I needed every spare centimetre it could give me. I shone my torch around, particularly on the dirt around me. I was no tracker, but I saw no evidence of anyone nearby. Nothing disturbed or broken. Just a plain forest floor covered in the dead leaves and sticks of winter, the dirt untouched.

"Hey, wait!"

My heart jumped into my throat. A girl. There was a girl up ahead. I caught only a glimpse, but it was enough, and there was no mistaking it. There was a girl, barefoot and in a white dress, running through the trees up ahead.

"Stop!"

I ran in her direction, forcing my way through tight spots in the trees and ignoring the branches grabbing for my face. The girl's footsteps hastened, and I with them. Finished, the string fell from my hand, and I stopped to look at it. The string or the girl. She was just up ahead. I could reach her in time. I could.

I ran as fast as my feet would take me, carrying me blindly through the trees.

"Please, stop! I just want to talk!"

But she didn't stop. The light from my torch highlighted the dirty soles of her feet as it thrashed wildly through the trees. The faster I ran, the faster she ran. I pushed through, no idea where the string was, but the girl was just there. I could almost reach out and touch her. A little faster and I would catch up. I could find out what was going on. Just a little more…

The footsteps stopped. The dry leaves and gravel fell silent and I skidded to a halt. I shone the light ahead of me, but the girl was gone. Nothing but trees. I turned back and shone the light in the other direction. The trees looked exactly the same. Which way had the girl gone? I couldn't tell anymore. Which way had I come from? My lungs burned and my heart pounded.

"Don't follow me."

'I'm sorry,' I thought. I did exactly what you told me not to do and now look at me. Lost in the middle of the woods on a wild goose chase. How was I supposed to get out now? I should have known something like this would happen. The forest wouldn't give its secrets up so easily, and in the back of my mind I knew it would try to tempt me, to lead me astray and pull me from the path. Like a fool I let it. I had no idea where I was, and no-one to blame but myself.

I felt a lump in my pocket. No, there was still one option left. The necklace. It would lead me to Keiko, wherever she was. It wasn't the best option, but it was a start. The forest was playing with me, drawing me further in, hoping I'd lose all sense of direction and get stuck there like the others. But I wasn't like the others. It would only take a moment. Just long enough to see where she was, and I could let go before the spirits closed in. It would be perfectly safe. Just a quick peek, at the very least to point me in the direction I should be going.

I took my glove off. I put my hand in my pocket and reached for the necklace. Just a peek. That was all.

"Ah!"

A pale face appeared before me. I tripped, landing against a thick tree. The girl didn't move. She stood ghostly still and pointed to the brush by her left. I lifted the torch with a shaky hand and she continued to stare into my eyes. Her gaze never wavered, nor did her arm. Yet as I raised the light to her face, she was gone.

A body lay face down in the dirt underneath the brush. Her feet were dirty and her dress stained. I turned her over and my heart dropped. The little girl from the man's photo. The girl who went missing without a word on her way to school.

"I'm so sorry..."

A noose lay on the ground next to her, cut in half, and as I shone the light across the ground something glittered. I leaned down and picked it up.

"Oh my god..."

Sayumi's brooch. The one and only keepsake she had of her mother. She wore it all the time and only took it off to sleep. She was here. There was no denying it; Sayumi was here in Kurohana Forest. My mind ran wild. Was she looking for the missing girls as well? When did she come to the forest? Was she still here? Did the forest try to confuse her as well and she was still running around, looking for a way out? Or perhaps...

I turned around and found myself face to face with the little girl again. She looked deep into my eyes, and for the first time I saw the blood dripping down from them. No icy-cold fingers gripped me, nor did she beg for help or make any attempt to grab me. She said only one thing.

"Run."

13

SOMETHING CRUNCHED NEARBY. I GRABBED Sayumi's brooch and took off running. The trees blurred together in an endless backdrop of bark and branches. I had no idea where the string was, or where I was, but in the moment it didn't matter. Something was close, something I didn't want to run into, and I needed to put as much distance between myself and it as possible.

"Shit!" The torch fell out of my hand and cracked on the hard ground below. There was no time to pick it up, nor time to worry about it. It made little difference as I ran anyway, and I relied upon my senses and the trees themselves to make my way forward.

The little girl was dead, and if the noose by her body was anything to go by, she was hung. I found it hard to believe that a young girl would find herself so deep in the woods, know how to fashion a noose from such thick rope, and be able to string it up over a tree branch to hang herself. It made no sense. Someone—or something—brought her here and killed her. Made it look like a suicide. But who? Why?

The footsteps in the distance grew closer. I ran and ran, shielding my face from the branches trying to claw it off, pushing through without regard for what stood before me. It didn't matter where I was going; escaping from whatever was pursuing me was of the utmost importance. Locating the exit was second. Somewhere in the distance wind chimes rattled. My heart skipped a beat. Wind chimes? It was winter, not summer. Not only that, but why were there wind chimes in the middle of the forest?

The vision. It came flooding back. When I held Keiko's necklace I heard wind chimes in the distance. But where were they coming from?

"Shit!"

I hit the ground with a loud thud. A thick, solid branch collided with my face, sending me sprawling. Pain shot up my side, and I scrambled to my feet in a daze. There was no time for rest. No time to feel the pain. My lungs and legs and ribs could burn later in the safety of my own home. I felt something beneath my fingers as I planted them into the dirt and my heart jumped for joy.

The string.

"No way."

Picking it up, I tugged on it and let it guide me back to safety. I was an anchor, and it was pulling me back to the ship. I ran as fast as my legs would take me and the footsteps behind me stopped. The chimes, however, grew angrier. They tinkled louder than ever, a cacophony of sound that made it difficult to think. But I didn't need to think. I pulled myself along the string, my body and mind focused on that one small thing. Follow the string. Get to safety. Worry about the rest later.

Laughter. A woman's laughter rang out in the distance, impossible to tell which direction it was coming from. Perhaps it was coming from all directions. I ran faster, my breath coming in ragged and my feet tripping over each other, sending me to my knees every few metres. Keep going, Mako. You're nearly there. I didn't know how far away I was, but what else could I tell myself?

The trees thinned, and all of a sudden the chimes stopped. Just like that. The forest fell silent, and the silence was deafening. I didn't dare stop, but I soon found myself back on the path leading out of the forest, and I ran until I reached the station and collapsed on the platform.

Safety. I had made it.

Keiko was in that forest, but she wasn't the only one. That man's daughter was also in there, lured by someone—or something—to her death among the trees. And Sayumi… That was the biggest mystery of all. Why was Sayumi in the forest? What was she doing in there, and why didn't she want me to know she was there in the first place?

I sat on the bench and looked up.

"What the…?"

The clock above the platform read 7:10 p.m. I shook my head. That was impossible. It couldn't be. How… I arrived at Kurohana Station shortly before 7 p.m. There was no way that in the time it took me to exit the station, enter the forest, get lost, find the little girl's body, find my way back to the string, and then get out of the forest again only 10 minutes had passed. It made no sense.

"What the hell is going on?"

The next train wasn't for another 20 minutes. The station was desolate; cold, empty, and devoid of life. Nearby animals avoided the area, and it was like the pile of concrete that made up the station itself didn't even want to be there anymore. 20 minutes until the next train. The forest loomed in the dark behind me. I feared that if I turned around, that would be the end of it. I wouldn't just see something that I shouldn't; sure, that alone was enough to send chills down my spine and cause my heart to sit tight in my throat, but somewhere, like a tingling on the back of my neck, I could feel it calling to me. I wasn't supposed to escape. I had cheated the forest of its prize. It didn't often give up its meals, and it wanted me back.

Sayumi was in there. I could get up, turn around, run back in and find her. I had her brooch. It was a direct line to her. I could find her in an instant. My fingers reached down into my pocket, fumbling for it. Grab it. Open yourself up and let go. Find her. Help her. She needs you. You're the only one who can help her. You know how dark it is in there, and she's all alone without anyone to trust, anyone to help.

Do it. Find her. Let us in.

I yanked my hand out of my pocket and shook my head. Cold tendrils snaked around my neck and down my back. They wrapped around my wrist and circled my ankles.

"Leave me alone!"

They weren't my thoughts, and the fact that I wanted them made them all the more dangerous. I couldn't turn around. I couldn't see what was standing there, waiting for me. Calling me back. If it was Sayumi, I didn't know what I'd do. No, that was a lie. I knew exactly what I would do, and that was why I couldn't turn around. Because it wouldn't be Sayumi. She was in there, that much I was certain of. But the thing waiting by the edge of the forest, calling to me like a siren zeroing in on its prey, that wasn't her. Using Sayumi's brooch, opening myself up to her, that was what the thing wanted. What the forest wanted. It would open me up as well, and once the spirits were let in, they would be near impossible to get back out. They would know me and they would be able to find me and no matter how long it took, they would bring me back.

I shook my head. "I'm sorry, Sayumi. I'm sorry…"

Just a little longer… Wherever she was, she had to hold out for just a little longer. I would find her, but the next time I entered the forest, I needed to be ready.

The cold tendrils withdrew. The clock ticked slowly, loudly, overhead.

Soon.

14

A QUICK STROLL WILL CLEAR my head and give me some time to sort out my thoughts. That's what I thought as I stepped outside into the cold winter air, but a large part of me just wanted to be around people. Any people. It didn't matter who, so long as they were alive and they were there.

The atmosphere in Matsuda Tea and Sweets felt different after the events of the last few days. It wasn't home anymore. I was a foreign body the building was trying to eject, the last hang-on of some virus it didn't want and was doing all in its power to destroy. The house was cold and uninviting. My footsteps echoed as I walked down the hall, but the sound was angry. *Get off my floorboards*, it screamed at me. The stairs groaned as I walked up them, and the darkness in Sayumi's room threatened to pull me in and never let go, a black hole of loneliness and confusion.

And my room. It was no longer my room. An

intruder had been in there, and a spirit or the house itself had repelled them, but now when I stepped inside, there was no longer a sense of comfort or warmth. That pleasant feeling like being wrapped in a soft blanket was gone, and instead it was like walking into an icy cave. *You're not wanted here. Get out.*

I couldn't get the images of the previous night out of my mind, nor the feeling of something crawling underneath my skin. Three things I knew for certain; first, Sayumi was in that forest. Her brooch remained safely in my pocket, wrapped up so I could avoid the temptation to dive into something I wasn't ready for; second, that man's daughter was also in the forest, but she was—unfortunately—already dead; and third, Keiko was also there. I didn't know where or if she was still alive, but I tried not to think about the alternative. My job was to find her. I intended to see that through, no matter the end result.

I should call Yasu and let him know, I thought. It was the middle of the day and he was likely at work. Perhaps later, just to keep him updated on what was going on. He didn't need the finer details and would probably be better off not knowing, but when I thought about Sayumi, and how I would feel if someone told me they had news about her, well, it was the least I could do.

A poster on the local police box caught my eye. It was fresh, the colours vivid and the paper shiny. It covered several older posters, many of whom were missing family members or pets. Something about this girl stood out. Underneath was the girl's age (twelve), the date she went missing (three days earlier), and where she was last seen (on her way to school in the morning). Just like the other girl. A classmate? At the very least they attended the same school, and the other girl's father mentioned she disappeared on her way to school as well. Behind the shiny new missing poster was another missing woman. This woman disappeared a month ago on her way home from work. Just like the other girls, she was on her way to or from somewhere and never reached her destination. She was never seen again. It was like they were disappearing into thin air.

Only they weren't. At least three of them were confirmed to be in Kurohana Forest. It wouldn't be too much of a stretch to believe these two girls were somewhere inside as well. But the one question that kept bothering me was 'why?' Why were they disappearing without a trace, and why there? Kurohana was hardly the only forest in the country known for its high rate of suicides. Kurohana was barely known outside the prefecture other than by those who had an interest in such things. And perhaps most importantly… why now? It wasn't unknown for a person to go missing every once in a while, but most showed up somewhere eventually, and it was rare for so many people to go missing at once.

I continued down the road. How many girls were missing in total? Were there others the police were unaware of yet? How many more would go missing until the forest had its fill? Would it continue to claim women indefinitely until it was stopped?

Clouds settled overhead, not threatening to rain but putting a damper on the mood. The town was grey and dreary. Shop doors and windows were shuttered against the cold. Wind picked up dead leaves, sending them flying into the air before landing once more in the gutter. The tiny, paved streets looked lovely and quaint in summer, but in winter they brought about a unique melancholy that longed for the colours of spring.

The library—in reality a two-story building that was thin enough to slot into the empty lot between the local-owned liquor store and a flower shop—was a few streets away from Matsuda Tea and Sweets. It wasn't much of a library, and calling it that felt strange and foreign. It housed public documents for the community, however, so perhaps it might reveal a little more about Kurohana Forest. There was a mystery waiting to be unravelled, and lives literally depended on it.

I stepped inside and out of the cold. A portly old man looked up from his book and considered me a few moments before speaking.

"Can I help you?"

I picked a leaf out of my hair and closed the door. "Hi, yes. Um, I was wondering if you had any information about Kurohana Forest?"

The man raised an eyebrow but said nothing.

"It's for a, um, project. I just wanted to learn a little more about the history of it."

He pointed to the stairs and a sign that read *LOCAL HISTORY - SECOND FLOOR.*

"If there's anything here, it'll be up there."

I bowed and smiled. "Thank you, sir. Thank

you."

I was halfway up the stairs when he called out behind me. "I'd be careful if I were you though."

I stopped and turned back. "Why's that?"

"Lots of young people visit Kurohana for fun and never seem to come back again..."

"Thank you for the concern." I bowed my head and disappeared upstairs. Book shelves were packed so tight that I could barely fit through them. Down the end of the second row I saw *LOCAL HISTORY* and I squeezed down the aisle sideways. I returned to the lone desk with an armful of books and folders and spread them out across the top.

City planning. Construction projects. Family registrars. Local folklore. Anything that looked like it might even vaguely reference Kurohana Forest, I brought out. There had to be something hidden within its history that hinted at what was going on. A construction project gone wrong, an unsolved murder, anything, and if there was, it would be in these files before me.

I sat down, turned on the desk lamp, and started flicking through the pages. I didn't know what I was expecting from the family registrar, but at the very least it showed that Kurohana Forest was not on private land, but public. The books on local folklore also proved to be surprisingly useless. One story involved a fat tanuki who, in times of old, was said to steal sake from the local merchants and retire to the forest to drink them. A traveller caught the tanuki unawares one day and he offered to share his stolen liquor with the man in exchange for his life. The man killed the tanuki, drank the liquor, and passed out in the river on the way to town. His body was found the next morning, wrinkled and dead and his belly looking not unlike that of the fat tanuki he had mercilessly slaughtered. It was the only mention of Kurohana Forest in local folklore, and it seemed unlikely that a drunk tanuki and sneaky traveller had anything to do with what was going on now. I wasn't even sure what the moral of the story was supposed to be. Don't steal? Don't drink other's stolen goods? I pushed the book away and grabbed the next one; construction projects.

I flicked through the pages; the sections were split up by year, then month, then day, detailing any construction projects undertaken in the town and the surrounding areas. Large letters under the NOVEMBER 1983 section drew my attention. My heart beat wildly.

KUROHANA SHRINE. CONSTRUCTION BEGINNING 11/11/83.

A shrine in the forest? That had to be it. It had to be connected somehow. I continued reading, jotting down notes in the pad I brought with me. The file contained the construction dates, including completion, who worked on the shrine, the companies that supplied the material, everything. Using that, I extracted every piece of information I could find from the other books, and finally found what I was looking for in a rather small and unassuming city pamphlet from the mid-1980s.

Built deep within Kurohana Forest, the

Kurohana Shrine is the pride of Shirotama Village. Construction of the shrine was completed in 1984 after many hardships, not least of which being the shrine's location; Kurohana Shrine can be found exactly 1,000 metres from the forest's edge, an auspicious number for such a treasured symbol of the community. Not only that, but the location Kurohana Shrine was built upon has long been claimed as a power spot by the village's locals, and the small temple that existed on the spot has been renovated and attached to the main shrine. For hundreds of years, people have travelled all around to visit this particular spot within Kurohana Forest, and now, the village of Shirotama is happy to share with them the Kurohana Shrine.

A shrine in the middle of the forest with a temple attached. Not unheard of, although it was increasingly rare in modern times. Something about the mixing of death with Shinto beliefs of cleanliness that many people didn't like. The original temple, which remained nameless in the documents, was built on what the locals called a "power spot." An area of the forest they went to in order to pray and receive energy. These also weren't uncommon, although I didn't place much faith in them. A power spot, a temple and a shrine. It was like the start of a bad joke.

I put the files back and returned with the pile of newspapers going all the way back to the early 1980s. It didn't take long to find what I was looking for: September 1986. Only two years after construction was completed there was an article about the decline of the shrine.

Kurohana Shrine, once the pride of Shirotama Village and the figurehead of their tourism campaigns, has officially been closed. Officials gave no reason as to why the shrine was closed, but locals have suggested the difficulty in reaching the shrine played a part.

"It's one thing to travel deep into the forest for a power spot, you know?" one man answered our reporters. "That's the type of thing you do maybe once a year, but to visit a shrine? I don't know what they were thinking."

"I tried to visit the shrine as often as I could when it first opened," another woman said. "But in the end, it was too difficult to get there. I had to drive to the station, take the train, and then hike through a kilometre of forest just to reach it. I heard they'll be finishing another new shrine inside the village soon. I'll just go there instead."

When The Shirotama Times asked officials what was to happen with the graveyard attached to the temple behind the shrine, one source who wished to remain anonymous said, "Nothing. The graves were there before the shrine and so they will remain there after."

Power spot. Temple. Shrine. Graveyard. The shrine was built to take advantage of the popularity of the power spot, but within a few short years the government realised the difficulty in reaching the shrine made it unpopular, and thus it was abandoned. Now there was news of a graveyard attached to the temple as well. Things were getting better and better.

I flicked through the rest of the newspapers, but there was little mention of Kurohana Shrine again. It sprung to life almost instantaneously and died again just as fast. An article from 1989 caught my attention, however, and I shoved it under the light.

Local Woman Goes Missing

A young woman, native to Shirotama Village and a former shrine maiden for the now-abandoned Kurohana Shrine, has gone missing. Police are looking for any clues as to her whereabouts.

"We were alerted to the woman's disappearance on the morning of the fourteenth. According to the woman's husband, after Kurohana Shrine closed down she continued to visit the graveyard by the attached temple to pay her respects to the dead. She has been doing so weekly, without fail, since the shrine closed down and she left to return to civilian life."

I grabbed more papers, scanning them for any news of the shrine maiden. This was it. I could hear the chimes ringing in the forest as though they were right behind me once more. This shrine maiden had something to do with the disappearances, I just had to figure out why. Adrenaline pushed me through, my eyes scanning over the text faster than I'd ever read before. I threw papers on the ground, my eyes trained for one thing, and one thing only.

I finally found it. Several months after the announcement of the shrine maiden's disappearance, there was a brief notice in the back of the paper.

A ceremony was held for the missing maiden of Kurohana Shrine. No body was recovered, but at her family's behest, a private ceremony was held in the family home. Those wishing to leave their condolences can visit the community hall during the next week to say their goodbyes.

They never found her body. She was angry. Perhaps something happened to her out there in the forest; perhaps not a drunk tanuki, but a stalker or a murderer while she was tending to the graves. Perhaps she was in the wrong place at the wrong time and bumped into a grave robber. Or perhaps she was injured and, so far from help, died of her wounds all alone, cold and in pain.

I put the papers away and checked that I had everything in my notes. The picture was already forming in my mind and I knew what I needed to do. I didn't want to, not after last time, but it had to be done. The shrine maiden wanted to be laid to rest. She was calling people to her; I didn't know how, but maybe they were related to the people buried in the graves. I didn't know. It didn't matter. She was calling them and, in her rage, keeping them there. She needed help, and Sayumi must have realised that. That was why she told me not to follow her. How stupid I was. She didn't want me tangled up in this mess that she thought she could handle alone.

I thanked the man on my way out the door and

ran down the street, an extra bounce in my step. I found what I needed, and I knew what I had to do. I would find the missing girls, I would find Sayumi, and I would help put the shrine maiden to rest.

Everything was going to be fine.

15

"HAVE YOU FOUND KEIKO YET? Do you know where she is?"

I didn't even have time to say hello before Yasu's voice assaulted me over the phone.

"Hello, uh, no, not yet. But I think I'm getting closer."

"You think?" His voice was so loud that I had to pull the phone away from my ear. "What do you mean, 'you think'?"

The sun was setting outside. I didn't have much time before I'd need to vacate the store, but I couldn't outright tell Yasu about what I'd seen. That his girlfriend was somewhere inside the supposedly cursed Kurohana Forest.

"I mean that I'm getting closer, but I don't have anything solid yet. If you give me a little more—"

"It's already been several days!" he screamed. I held my tongue. His fiancée was missing, and I understood all too well how it felt to have a loved one suddenly up and disappear. He was upset. He had every right to be.

"Sir, please—"

"Do you know how it feels?" he interrupted me again, his voice hoarse. "Every night when I climb into bed she's not there, but I can still smell her. I fall asleep not knowing whether she's alive or dead. Not knowing whether she's sick, or injured, or in pain. I don't know if someone kidnapped her and is torturing her in a dark basement somewhere, or if she's lying dead in a ditch, lost and waiting for someone to bring her home. I wake up and the scent of her is still there. I reach out but... there's nothing. She's gone. Every time I open my eyes and she's not there I'm brought back to reality once more. Do you know how that feels? Do you?"

"I understand, sir, I do, but—"

"How could you?"

I stopped. "I'm sorry?"

"How could you understand what it's like? Have you lost a boyfriend? A lover? How do you know what I'm feeling right this very moment?"

He's in pain, I reminded myself. He's lashing out at whatever he can because that's the only reaction he knows. It's not personal.

"I lost my parents," I said. "They were murdered right in front of me."

"Then you understand nothing."

That hurt more than I wanted to let on, but I pushed the feelings aside. He was like a wounded cobra trapped in a cage, and he would continue to lash out at anything and everything until his energy was spent.

"I just… I need you to find her."

"I'm doing my best, sir."

"Do you have any idea? Any idea at all where she might be?"

Yes. Trapped in a cursed forest. Not that I could tell him that.

"I'm not sure, but I'm doing everything I can to find her."

He fell silent. The sun was disappearing behind the trees outside and the streetlights flickered on. I didn't have much time, but it would be rude to hang up on him.

"I'll make sure to call you first thing the moment I know something. Don't worry. Please."

"I just… I miss her."

"I know."

"I'm sorry."

"It's fine, sir. Really. I understand."

He sniffled. "Sometimes I think I see her. I wake up and she's standing by the end of the bed, looking down at me. My heart starts pounding, like, she's come back! She's finally come back! But when I turn the light on, she's gone. Or she was never really there to begin with. I don't know. Maybe it's all just a dream. A horrible, bad dream."

Or maybe it wasn't.

"Does she ever… say anything when you see her?"

"No. At least, I don't think so. It's too dark to see clearly, and I don't remember hearing her say anything. She's just standing there. Looking at me."

"Have you seen her anywhere else?"

"No. Does it mean anything?" His voice was

suddenly full of hope. He was so desperate that he'd grab at any straw presented to him, no matter what it was.

"It means you miss her." He fell silent. The sun faded from view and my skin began to crawl. "But if anything else comes up, anything at all, please give me a call, okay?"

"Yeah. Sure. Of course. Thank you."

"We'll find her. Don't worry. I will call you the moment I know anything myself." Anything that wouldn't send him running to his death. I needed more time. There was still so much I didn't understand about the situation, not to mention whether Keiko was still alive or not.

"Thank you. I'll call again soon."

"Okay. Good night."

I hung up and ran over to the front door, locking it. I didn't know why I bothered; anyone stupid enough to come into the store after dark wouldn't be leaving again. When Sayumi first told me not to venture in the store after dark, I asked her if anyone else ever had. "Yes," she said. "A colleague of my grandfather's. I was only young at the time, perhaps five or six-years-old. He owed my grandfather some money and came around to argue about it. He was drunk, of course. He had a problem with drink and gambling. He beat on the door, over and over, until my grandfather yelled from upstairs for him to go away. He'd deal with him in the morning. All the screaming woke me up. I stumbled into the hall and I heard the sound of glass smashing downstairs; turned out he'd taken a stone and broken the front door window glass. He opened the door and came into the store screaming. My grandmother came running out and put me back to bed. She stayed with me, telling me stories, until I fell asleep again. The store was closed the next day and my grandmother took me out to the park while grandfather 'cleaned things up.' By cleaning she meant the man's body. They found him torn to shreds. Officially it was a wild animal attack, although the police could offer no clue as what animal it was. My grandfather knew better. As did the chief. He was aware of the strange happenings around town, and particularly our house. That was the end of that, and whenever I brought up the store after dark, they gently reminded me of what would happen should I errantly stray."

A chill ran down my spine. I hurried out, closing the door to the hall behind me. The back door was tied closed with string. The repairman was busy and wouldn't be out for another few days, he said. Nowhere was safe anymore.

Nowhere.

16

THE DOORBELL TINKLED THE NEXT morning and a familiar face entered the store. Mr Fujita, a jolly old man and one of the store regulars.

"Welcome!"

"Ah, hello dear. How are things?"

"Good, sir, thank you."

He walked over to the counter and put his hands down on the edge. "It's a little sudden, but I don't suppose Ms Matsuda is in?"

I shook my head. "I'm terribly sorry, she's still on her vacation."

He clucked in disappointment. "Ah, that sure is a shame. My wife is having a little get-together this weekend, and she was hoping Ms Matsuda would join and make some of her famous matcha for them. Do you know when she'll be back?"

"She should be back in another week or so." The lie rolled off my tongue from all the practice it'd been getting lately. "I'll make sure to let her know that Mrs Fujita is looking forward to seeing her again."

The man waved it away. "Ah, it's no bother. My wife is just fussy and too lazy to learn how to make the tea herself. I keep telling her it's not that difficult. You stick the whisk in and stir and voila, you have tea. But she's all 'Nooo, first you must do this, and then you have to do this, and if you don't turn the cup in this direction this many times, then it doesn't taste as good, and…'"

I smiled as he continued his rant. In some households, tea was very serious business, apparently.

"Anyway, never mind. How are you going, Mako? You're growing up into such a beautiful young woman, how are you not beating the men off with sticks?" Mr Fujita always called me by my first name. It didn't bother me; on the contrary, he was like the kindly old grandfather I never had. It was welcoming more than condescending, but the words sent a shiver down my spine, regardless. They reminded me of Hiroshi. I hadn't seen the delivery guy for several days.

"I'm fine, thank you, Mr Fujita. I'm looking forward to Ms Matsuda's return. The store can get a little stressful when it's just me running it."

He laughed, a booming sound that filled the room. "Oho, I bet, if your customers are anything like my wife. No special man in your life yet?"

"No, sir." I dared not tell him about the problems with Hiroshi. Mr Fujita was a friendly old man, but also robust for his age and a little rough around the edges. The last thing we needed was him trying to rough up a delivery driver when there was no hard evidence of any wrongdoing.

"You know, I still remember the first time I met you. You were this tiny, thin little girl cowering in the corner. That corner, right there." He pointed behind me, past the register. "You could barely speak and never looked up from your long hair draped over your face. You were like that every time I came in. Bless Ms Matsuda for all the good work she does helping people around the community, but if I'm entirely honest, her best work was you. Look at you now."

I didn't know how to respond to that. I tried not to think of my early days in the store, when Sayumi took me in because I was too old for foster care and had no family left to stay with. Well, I did have a cousin a few hours away, but she was only a few years older than myself and in no position to take care of me.

"T-Thank you, sir," I said.

"A terrible thing that happened to your parents, truly terrible," he continued. "And they never found who did it, did they?"

"No, sir."

"That just…" He hesitated a moment and clenched a fist. "That just boils my blood. Shirotama has always been such a nice village, and for something like that to happen, and for no-one to ever be charged for it, well…" He turned to look at me again. "I'm sorry, child. I truly am."

I shook my head furiously. No-one was charged for their murder because there was no-one to charge. Sayumi was the only person other than myself who knew the truth. The rumours that spread around town in the days and weeks following the brutal deaths of my parents said that a man sneaked in during the night and stabbed them to death. He was so violent in his attack that there was little left to identify the bodies when he was done. But there was no man. My parents' deaths were my fault. I was playing around with things I shouldn't have. Testing my limits. I was angry and upset. They treated me like a child and I was determined to prove I wasn't.

I went down to my family's altar room and opened the small cupboard containing my grandparents' remains. Neither my mother nor my father ever spoke of them, nor of what happened to them. I wanted to find out for myself and grabbed the urn containing my grandfather's ashes.

It turned out there was a good reason they never told me about my grandparents. My grandfather in particular. The moment I focused on his urn, and on the only image I had of him in my mind—the photo of him in the very same altar—I was flooded with evil. That was the only way I could describe it. The urn wasn't just connected to him; it *was* him. His spirit was resting somewhere—I didn't know whether it was peacefully, but it was resting—and I called him back. It wasn't just him, however. I had no idea what I was doing, I just knew that I could see things when I picked up objects and focused on them. That day I unleashed a wave of evil into our house. Not just my grandfather, but swarms of spirits I couldn't control and couldn't stop. They spotted me and they followed me back. When the police found me the next morning covered in the blood of my parents and a fire raging upstairs, they took me in and declared the house a crime scene. It was a crime scene alright, but not of the human kind. I had no idea where the spirits went after they were done slaughtering my parents, nor why they left me alive and alone with their mangled, broken corpses, but it didn't take long for news to spread. I was the lone survivor of the 'red room.' They put the fire out, but they could never get the blood out of the floor or walls. In the end, they demolished the house and the empty lot was left to me in my father's will. I never wanted to step foot on it again.

"Anyway," Mr Fujita interrupted my trip down memory lane, "there's been a lot of strange things going on around town lately, don't you think?"

"What do you mean?"

"Well, I was talking to my neighbour the other day, and his daughter was supposed to come and visit him for his birthday last week. Only she never showed up."

My heart skipped a beat. "W-Was she okay?"

Mr Fujita shook his head, his eyes downcast. "They found her the next day by the river just outside town. Strangled and…" His voice trailed off. He didn't need to say the rest. I could guess.

"That's terrible." And it was happening with increasing frequency, it seemed. What was going on?

"They found her car sitting in a convenience store parking lot. The officers said it was the second body they'd found like that in the last month."

Wait, so the girl wasn't anywhere near Kurohana

Forest, and she wasn't a lone victim either?

"What do you mean, she was the second they found like that? I haven't heard anything about it."

Mr Fujita shrugged. "I think they probably don't want the media to know about it yet. They don't want people to panic or something. Stupid, if you ask me. People deserve to know. People have the right to protect themselves."

I was in over my head. So much was going on that I didn't understand.

"Well, I better at least grab some tea while I'm here so my wife doesn't beat me when I get home." Mr Fujita winked with a devilish smile and grabbed a few bags of matcha powder. "You give Ms Matsuda my best when she returns and tell her she owes me a free dinner for all the nagging I've had to put up with from my bored wife since she's been gone."

I forced a smile on my lips and nodded. "Yes, Mr Fujita. Of course." I gave him his change, and he held a hand up.

"You take care, Mako. It's a dangerous world out there. If you see or hear anything suspicious, you call the police at once, okay?"

"Yes, sir."

"You're a good kid. Be careful."

My heart sank as he left and silence fell over the store once more.

17

MRS TAMITA'S PHOTO STARED BACK at me from the desk. Another uneventful day had passed, but that set my nerves even more on edge. Like things were building in the background, getting ready to explode before I was able to do anything to stop it. Well, I wouldn't let that happen. I could do this. The power was within me; I didn't need help. It was a simple photo album, and after searching for it several times, I finally got a hit. This time I knew what to look for and how to find it again.

I could do it. I couldn't put it off any longer.

A quick in and out; find the location of the album and then come back. I was no chicken and there was nothing to fear. It would be easier now that I knew what I was looking for and not being pulled to and fro by everything else in the photo. I'd find it before anything else found me. I was a professional, and this was an easy job. A quick victory would be a nice boost to my confidence after the last few days. I grabbed the photo and allowed myself to fall in. The familiar colours and sounds swirled around me until the image before my eyes settled.

An old woman was praying in front of an altar. Mrs Tamita. A man stood in the corner, watching her. Mr Tamita. He hadn't moved on. He was still there, watching over his wife. Why hadn't he moved on? Sadness. He couldn't move on. The feelings washed over me. The love he felt for his wife. His inability to leave her when she was in so much pain. Their memories. They weren't much, but in her old age, they were all she had. Mrs Tamita's shoulders heaved as she wept. Mr Tamita pointed outside.

I was in a creek. It was too small to be a river, but I didn't recognise it. Litter covered the banks on either side, and two small school children ran by in uniform. A chill settled over my skin. It started by my ankles and crawled, wrapping itself around my calves, then around my knees and up my legs. I called out to the children, but they couldn't hear me. Of course they couldn't; I wasn't there. It wasn't even the present. At least, I didn't think so.

Incorporeal forms rose from the water. Not darkness, not light, just forms. Invisible to the naked eye, but blinding to mine. More rose from the mud on the banks. For how bright they were to my eyes, I must have been even more blinding to them. They trudged through the mud and crawled through the water. More and more rose, making their way in my direction like moths to the flame. The chill wrapped around my stomach and snaked up my arms.

"Hey!" I called out, but the children laughed and ran past us. "Hey!" One stopped for a moment by the banks of the creek and my heart jumped. "Do you know—" The kid tied his shoelace and then ran to catch up with his friend. My heart sank as the chill rose to my neck. I tried to shake it off, but it clung tighter.

"Leave me alone!"

More forms were rising. There was no sign of the photo album. Why was I there? I searched frantically through the litter on the shore, frozen to the spot as my eyes darted around the blinding lights crawling towards me. It had to be there, but why couldn't I see it? It should have been brighter than anything else. I knew what it looked like now; not its physical form, but its spiritual. The figures around me were too bright. They were blocking not only the album but everything else from view as well.

I pulled at my own legs, determined to move. "Come on!" They were getting closer. The chill grabbed at the back of my neck, sliding around to the front of my face. "Get off me!"

A presence behind me made the hairs on my body stand on end. For a moment the figures stopped, and I was free. They didn't back away, but I feared turning around to see what made them stop in their tracks. I swallowed and time seemed to go still. I turned, slowly, unsure of what I might see and prepared myself to run just in case.

The figures swarmed me. The moment my eyes were off them they fell upon me, all over me, dragging me down with them into the cold watery depths below.

"No!"

I let go and was back in my room. Sweat poured down my brow despite the cold of the room and the goosebumps on my arms. The photo sat on the middle of the desk, nothing out of the ordinary. I wiped my forehead and waited for my breathing to calm down. What had gone wrong? The album was there somewhere. I wouldn't have been there if it wasn't. What was I missing?

I should make a note, I thought, and I remembered the emblem on the child's school uniform. Grabbing a piece of paper, I scribbled it down the best I could. I'd have to look it up later; it wasn't immediately familiar to me, and neither were the surroundings.

The hairs on the back of my neck continued to prickle. Something was in the room. Did I bring it back with me? No. I broke away in time. Nothing could have followed. I put my hands on the desk and took a deep breath. One of the techniques Sayumi told me to use in times of stress. "Sometimes you'll see things that aren't really there. It's okay. It's just a residual effect, and with enough time, you'll be able to tell the difference between what's real, and what's simply lingering."

I turned. Nothing was there. I let the breath out and laughed. Just a lingering aftereffect. Of course my nerves were on edge. I turned back to the desk and the old man's face was looking right at me.

"Quickly!" he screamed.

18

NIGHTMARES PLAGUED MY SLEEP. SPIRITS I couldn't see consumed me. I was blind to them, unable to see what was pulling me down, dragging me into the depths and drowning me. I couldn't feel them, but they were there. They were everywhere, and I was alone.

My eyes flung open and faces looked down on me. They weren't faces I recognised, and it took me a few moments to realise why. They weren't faces—not how we recognised them, anyway. They were darkness, unable to remember what they looked like in life and thus stuck formless in death. I fumbled for the lamp and pulled the string; light filled the room, and they were gone. Dirty, wet footprints stained the carpet where they once stood, and I turned as heavy rain pelted the window outside. Another storm. The room was cold, even more so than usual. I didn't like to use the heater; cold was something I grew used to over the years and it was another unnecessary expense, but I plugged it in and warmed myself before it.

It took me a few minutes to realise that something was banging downstairs as well. The storefront? I shook my head and rubbed my hands for heat. If someone was down there at this time of night, that wasn't my business. And if it wasn't a someone, but a something, well… that was *really* not my business.

Yet the banging continued unabated, growing more frequent and violent. "Go away!" I yelled, feeling the icy grip of winter ignore the heater before me. The banging continued, on and on, until finally it became too much. I threw the door open, anger propelling me forward, and stormed past Sayumi's open bedroom door.

"I said go away!"

Lightning flashed and several shadows appeared at the bottom of the stairs.

"I have nothing to do with you. Leave!" I stomped down the stairs, not really sure what I planned to do once I got there; it wasn't like I could forcibly shove them out the door or even punch them in the face like I wanted to, but I couldn't just stand at the top of the stairs and scream at shadows all night. "This isn't your place and I can't help you, so go!"

They were gone by the time I reached the bottom, and the back door flapped open and shut in the breeze. The broken lock… A large puddle of water was forming beneath the door and I sighed in relief. That would explain the cold and the banging. I retrieved some rope from the storage cupboard and tied it around the remains of the handle, looping it back around the cupboard to keep it closed. It would have to do until morning. The noise stopped, and I made a mental note to call the repairman again the next day. In the meantime that mess wasn't going to clean itself. I grabbed a mop, relieved that a puddle of water was the only thing I had to deal with.

Something banged upstairs and anger flared once more. "Oh, come on." I threw the mop down and leapt up the stairs, two at a time. The window in Sayumi's room was open, the curtain billowing wildly in the wind as rain poured in.

"Oh no!"

I ran in without thought and pulled it closed. A few items on her bedside table were wet, but there otherwise wasn't too much damage. I stopped to take it all in. The room still smelt like her; vanilla and lavender, her favourite scents. You could smell them a few moments before she entered the room, and a few moments after she exited as well. It brought with it a sense of calm. Of warmth and security and… love.

I dropped to my knees, and the tears poured forth before I could stop them. I hadn't allowed myself to cry or to feel anything that might suggest that Sayumi was gone and never coming back. The thought was forbidden, pushed from my mind before I could ever explore the possibilities of what it meant. She was on a job. It wasn't the first time. She'd be back.

I cried. The feelings washed over me and consumed me and I let them. I missed her. The house was so cold and lonely without her presence.

She was a shining star in a cold night, and now that she was gone it was dark and I was all alone. I was scared. Sayumi always knew what she was doing, and she was gentle in her guidance. She never led me astray and she never let anything hurt me. She shielded me from the horrors lurking in the darkness the best she could, and when things got too much, she was always there lending a shoulder to cry on.

"I… I don't know what to do, Sayumi." The sound of my voice in her empty room filled me with a sadness I didn't know I could feel. The world had moved on and forgotten me. I was all alone and left to fend for myself, blind and scared in the dark. "Why? Why did you leave me here? Why, you of all people… you know how I feel about…" my voice choked up "…about being left behind…"

A book fell off Sayumi's desk and landed on the floor with a thud. I got to my feet and picked it up. A piece of paper fell out and floated to the floor.

It was a map. A map of Kurohana Forest written in Sayumi's handwriting. Kurohana Station was there, the outline of the forest, and there was a large X in the middle with several landmarks marked along the way. Large letters stood out beneath the X.

KUROHANA SHRINE.

This was it. Proof that Sayumi was working on the same thing, and she was several weeks ahead of me. A crude drawing of a shrine maiden floated next to the shrine. I was right. It was the shrine maiden after all. Sayumi went to the forest in an attempt to appease the maiden and stop the disappearances and ended up disappearing herself.

Sayumi was in trouble. I had to help her before it was too late.

19

THE DOWNSTAIRS PHONE DREW ME from my revelry the next morning. I picked it up on the second ring.

"Matsuda Tea and Sweets."

"Mako?"

My heart jumped. A voice I hadn't heard in a long time replied. Possibly the voice I needed to hear most.

"Megu?"

"Oh thank god, you haven't changed numbers! I was worried that maybe you moved and didn't tell me, or maybe Ms Matsuda changed the number, or—"

"How are you?" It was so good to hear her voice again. The only blood relative I had left in the world. We didn't see each other often, and our contact was usually kept to holidays or big events, but in that moment, Megu's voice was the one I needed to hear most. I missed her.

"I'm… yeah. Okay, I guess," she replied. "A lot

of stuff's been going on here. I don't even know where to begin…"

"Stuff like what?"

Megu laughed, a sad, pitiable sound.

"Are you okay?"

"Yeah, no. Maybe. I don't know. I… I met this girl."

"Okay…"

"And there was a bunch of things… you know…"

I didn't know, but I nodded anyway. She couldn't see me, but it was a habit.

"Anyway, to cut a very long story short, it turns out she's… different."

I wasn't following. "Different how?"

"Like you. I think. Maybe. I don't… Help me out here, Mako."

Megu was as scatter-brained as always. "Megu, I have no idea what you're talking about."

She sighed. The sound brought a smile to my lips. She was flustered and terrible at hiding it. "I met this girl. She's very cute. But something was chasing her. Or at least, we thought something was chasing her…"

"Okay…"

"I tried to help her. I thought it was a ghost or something, or maybe something her father conjured. I don't know how these things work, that was always your thing. But anyway, it's not a ghost. Not really. I don't think so. It was always around her, or connected to her, or inside her, or—"

"Sounds like an *ikiryo*."

There was silence on the other end. "A what

now?"

"Ikiryo. A living spirit. You're right, it's not a ghost, not really. Not of a dead person, anyway. It's the spirit of someone who's still alive."

"…Huh. That actually makes a lot of sense now."

I tried to hide my smile. Megu was older than me, but she always reminded me of a younger sister. "An ikiryo usually comes about to seek vengeance or revenge for something done to the person in question. They're rare, but they can be extremely powerful."

Megu snorted. "Yeah, no kidding…"

"So this girl's cute, huh?"

I could hear Megu blushing from several prefectures away. "Maybe. Shut up. So anyway, putting that aside for the moment, how are things with you? I haven't heard from you in a while."

The store was empty. Not like talking to my one and only cousin for a few more minutes would do any harm, and maybe she could help the storm that was brewing in my heart.

"Sayumi's missing."

"What?" Sayumi was always kind to Megu, and Megu looked up to her like an aunt.

"She left a few weeks ago. She told me she was going out on a job and not to follow, but that was the last I heard of her. Since then… I don't know, Megu. People have been going missing around town, and a man came to me to help find his missing girlfriend."

"Okay…"

"So I agreed to help, and there's this forest

nearby that… that I think is haunted.”

“Oh. Eww. That’s… no thank you. I’m sorry.”

I picked up a pen and scribbled mindlessly on the piece of paper before me.

“And ever since Sayumi left, the house has been… different. It’s always been a little different, you know? But now… I don’t know anymore. I have to bring her back, and I’m scared.” It felt odd to say the words out loud. It was like admitting it to the world at large, and now I would be held accountable to those words.

“Are you okay? Do you need me to come down there?” The concern in her voice was evident, and it was enough to embolden me.

“No, Megu. It’s okay. Thank you. You sound like you have enough on your plate, anyway.”

“I mean, we can come down there together. Me and Aya. If you want.”

“Her name’s Aya?”

Megu fell silent for a moment, like she’d been caught out. “I think you’ll like her. She’s quiet and emotionally unavailable, just like you.”

I snorted despite myself. “Did you just make a joke at my expense?”

“Did it help?” Her voice was hopeful.

I sighed. “Not really, but I appreciate the attempt.”

“Seriously, Mako. You don’t need to do this alone. I mean, I can’t be there in the next ten minutes or anything, but I can make arrangements to come down. I don’t think I’ll be much help, I’m useless when it comes to this kinda stuff… or most stuff… but Aya…”

"It's fine, Megu. Really. But thank you."

An awkward silence filled the air again. An old couple walked past the store. I waited to see if they would enter, but they continued on their way.

"When you said the house was… strange… you mean like that whole 'no entering the store after dark' business?"

I continued scribbling on the paper. "No, not that. Well, strange things have been happening there too, but… I honestly don't know, Megu. This is the one place I can usually be at ease. I don't see anything here, and I think that's because of the spirits in the store after dark. But lately… Well, they've been invading the second floor as well. I don't know if it's the same spirits, or different ones, but—"

"The house is haunted?" Megu answered for me.

"I guess."

"Ugh, I don't know how you could live there to begin with. All those ghosts downstairs every night, why doesn't Sayumi do anything to get rid of them?"

To that, I honestly didn't know the answer. "I think she tried, a while ago, but nothing worked. When she realised it kept other spirits away, however, she stopped trying. It's like leaving a spider be so it'll kill the household bugs, you know? You don't touch it, it doesn't touch you, but it keeps the other pests away."

"Like a guard dog?"

"Yeah."

"A guard dog that could rip your face off at any moment?"

"…Yeah."

When she put it that way… "As long as we don't come down into the store after dark, it's fine. And if I have to share a space with them so I don't have to see other spirits all the time, well that's worth it for me."

"You're far braver than I could ever be."

"Says the girl threatening to bring an ikiryo to my doorstep."

Megu scoffed. "To help!"

"Remember that guard dog? That's a good analogy for your ikiryo friend as well."

"Yeah. Well. We're working on it."

I snickered. "We?"

"Well, she's working on it. I'm there for support."

"Uh huh."

"Shut up."

I missed Megu.

"And some delivery guy has been hassling me as well. Apparently he's been harassing several women around town. It never rains but pours, huh?" It felt nice to get everything off my chest, and I didn't have to pretend around Megu. She was unaware of the exact circumstances of my parents' deaths, but she otherwise knew all about me. What I could do and what I could see. She was the only person other than Sayumi that I could trust.

"What?" she screamed. I pulled the phone away from my ear. "Go to the police! Right now!"

"I can't," I replied, bringing the receiver back. "He technically hasn't done anything that's a crime yet. Well, I'm fairly certain he broke into the house the other night, but I don't have any proof of that either."

"What?" The scream got louder. "I'm coming down there right now!"

"No, Megu, please. It's fine. I'm handling things." I really wasn't handling things, but I didn't want to drag her into it as well. "The house dealt with him, anyway." I didn't know how else to explain it. Something happened, there was a scream, and then someone—most likely Hiroshi—broke out the back door and fled into the night.

"Mako."

"What?"

"I'm coming to see you."

"No. I'm fine, really. I just needed to get all of that off my chest."

"Mako."

"What?"

"I love you."

"I love you, too."

"But I'm still coming to see you."

I sighed.

"Keep all your doors locked and make sure you have the police on speed dial, okay?"

"Megu, it's not that—"

"Okay?" she interrupted me. There was no getting out of this one.

"I'll be there in a few days. I'd be there right this instant if I could, but there's some stuff I need to sort out here first."

"You really don't have to."

"I insist. And I'll bring my ikiryo friend with me. We'll bust down some asses, ghost and otherwise."

I smiled. There would be no arguing with her. She was nothing if not stubborn. "Thank you, Megu."

"You stay safe. We'll be there soon."

I hung up the phone and looked down at the notepad I was scribbling on. A shrine maiden was looking back at me, smiling. I tore the page out and threw it in the bin, my heart pounding wildly. A noise outside the store drew my attention back. A delivery truck pulled up and another familiar face stepped out.

20

HE WAS BACK. HIROSHI. HE stood in front of the store and glowered through the window, several boxes on his trolley. He raised a hand and rapped twice, then waited with his hands crossed in front of him.

"Good morning." It didn't feel like a good morning, and the expression on his face agreed with my sentiments.

"Delivery." He held his clipboard out for me to sign. No 'good morning' or 'how are you?' No invasive questions into the state of my loneliness or invitations to lunch. He wouldn't even look at me and turned his gaze to the roof as I took the clipboard from him.

"That's a nasty cut on your face there," I said, scribbling my name and handing the clipboard back. A large cut ran down the length of his cheek, mostly covered by small bandages. Anger flared in his eyes momentarily, a sudden fire roaring to life. He opened his mouth to say something, but then closed it and clenched his jaw. His eyes darted around and he looked over my shoulder before swallowing. The fire was replaced with fear.

"A fishing accident," he said, putting the clipboard back in his truck and waiting for me to open the door to let him in with the boxes.

"A fishing accident?" It was difficult to hide the disbelief in my voice and not laugh in his face.

"A fishing accident. Now, if you could just open the door and let me in so I can deliver these boxes and get back to work."

I opened the door and he rolled the boxes in. I pointed the usual corner and returned to the front counter. There was no friendly chit-chat, no leaning on the counter or picking up goods he didn't intend to buy. All of a sudden, Hiroshi the Delivery Guy was all business. He unloaded the boxes and then pulled a smaller package out of his pocket.

"Oh, I forgot this one." He put it down on the counter. This one was addressed to Sayumi personally, not the store. Curiosity burned, but I put it aside and thanked the man. He looked at me a few more moments, several emotions fleeting through his eyes like he wasn't sure what to feel or how to say it. Anger. Confusion. Fear. He unconsciously touched his cheek, and I decided to do something I'd never done before. I didn't know if it would work, but I figured there wouldn't be any harm in trying. Probably, anyway.

I reached forward and grabbed his wrist. I focused on the store itself, but it was too broad. Colours swirled everywhere and sounds fought each other for dominance. He came to the store all the time; it wasn't specific enough. I needed something better. The pen on my desk. Yes. I focused on the pen.

The colours focused and the sounds quietened. I was in my room. He was in my room. Hiroshi the Delivery Guy was standing in front of my desk, rifling through it, looking for something. I couldn't tell what, but the emotions were overwhelming. Anger. Lust. Rage. Humiliation. Panic. I rejected him and he wanted to teach me a lesson. He knew I was alone and he didn't want to hurt me—much, anyway—but a lesson had to be learnt and his feelings respected.

Two figures materialised beside the desk. The pen rose. Hiroshi realised too late. He ducked to the side and it slashed his cheek. He screamed and fled the room. A boot connected with the back door and he was outside. He was free.

I let go and Hiroshi yanked his arm back like I'd just stabbed him with hot pokers.

"W-What the fuck was that?"

Did he see it too? I'd only ever tried it with objects connected to people, not people connected to objects.

"I..."

"You crazy bitch!"

He backed away, bumping into a shelf and knocking some bags of tea onto the ground.

"It was you." There was no point in either of us pretending otherwise. "You were here, the other night. You were in my room."

"Y-You're crazy. I don't know what you're

talking about, but if you touch me again, I'm calling the police!"

"You're calling the police?" I laughed in disbelief. "You break into my house, my store, you sneak into my room and, and what? You plan to make me pay for not going out with you?" He continued to back away. "What exactly were you planning to do, huh? Maybe slap me around a little to prove a point? Tie me up and leave me there?" I moved around the counter and he backed up into the door, knocking his trolley over. "Or maybe something else. That's it, isn't it? I said no and refused to play your little games, so you were just going to take what you wanted anyway like some spoilt little child."

"You're insane!" His lips quivered and he fumbled to pick the trolley up, placing it between us for safety. "A-All of you are the same. Stay away!"

"Perhaps you should have taken your own advice before breaking into my house and leaving your DNA everywhere. Like your blood on my pen."

His face said it all. Why didn't I think of that before? In my fear it had completely escaped my mind. His blood was on my pen. I did have evidence. It was right up there in my desk. Hiroshi swallowed and leapt for the door handle, jiggling it over and over. It refused to open. He turned back to look at me. "Now you're locking me in? Is that what this is? You think this is funny?"

I held my hands up in the air. "I was behind the counter all this time. You saw me with your own two eyes, Hiroshi." He flinched at hearing his name. "Yes, Hiroshi, I do know your name. You told me several times, and it's right there on your name tag." He looked down and blushed. "And yes, you better believe I'll be filing a report, not only with the police but with your company as well. I hope you didn't like delivering because I'm pretty sure your days as a delivery driver are numbered."

He jiggled the door handle again furiously. "What the hell? Let me out of here!"

I walked over and Hiroshi stumbled back, giving me a wide berth. I turned the handle and the door opened. He slinked through the open space with his trolley, threw it into the back of his truck, and then jumped inside. He gave me one last glance before taking off, the fear plain in his eyes.

I turned back to the handle. The lock was a simple knob on the back, and it was still in the unlocked position. The door wasn't the thing keeping him in the store. Something else was. I returned to the front counter and sat down. The antique clock above my head ticked. Tick. Tock.

Silence filled the room.

21

I RETREATED TO MY ROOM after work. The brief rush of power I felt when I grabbed Hiroshi's arm was long gone, and as darkness settled over the house, a familiar fear returned with it.

Two figures were in my room when Hiroshi broke in. Two figures I had never seen before. They were in my room. Not the storefront, not Sayumi's room. My room. It wasn't my safe space anymore, and that unnerved me more than anything. They must have followed me back, but from where? The album? Keiko? The forest?

Memories of Kurohana came flooding back. I had to go back, but every bone in my body screamed that it was wrong. Stay away; far, far away. Nothing good is waiting in that forest and nothing good will come from it either. Just carry on with your life like you never heard about it and that will be the end of it.

But I couldn't do that. I pulled Sayumi's brooch

out of my pocket and lay it on the desk before me. There was no way I could ignore what was going on there; not with how much I knew, and what was at stake. Yes, Sayumi was there, that much was undeniable. I found her brooch on the forest floor, and her room had presented me with a map she was working on before she left. A map that laid out the location of Kurohana Shrine, the same conclusion my research had led me to. She was there, and I had to find her and bring her back, but that wasn't all. That little girl's father deserved to know where she was. I couldn't tell him, not yet. It wasn't safe to enter the forest, and without proof, well… it was more unnecessary worry that he didn't need right now. He deserved to know, but only once it was safe. And Keiko. I didn't know whether she was dead or alive, but she was in there, and if she was alive, I had to do everything in my power to get her out safely as well.

They weren't the only ones, however. The girls on the posters outside the police box. The rumours around town of other girls gone missing. For some reason, the disappearances were increasing in frequency, and they wouldn't stop until someone laid the shrine maiden's spirit to rest.

The map sat safely in my desk drawer with Keiko's photo and necklace. Only the brooch remained on the desk, its bright blue stone staring back at me like a lost and lonely eye. What must it have seen? What secrets lay in its depths? I took my gloves off and laid them on the side of the desk. I wanted nothing more than to grab the brooch and find Sayumi immediately, run to the forest and drag her back home. Yet fear ran deep. Something else was in that forest, and that thing might very well find me the instant I tried to find her. The hunter becomes the hunted. That was how the saying went, right?

The forest was evil. Perhaps it was once a power spot, a location of spiritual power that it granted upon those who visited, but now… something had changed. The energy was corrupted. Tainted. Evil.

Screw it. I had to know.

"I'm sorry, Sayumi."

I grabbed the brooch before I could talk myself out of it again and squeezed my eyes shut.

A dark forest floor, covered in dry leaves and sticks. Endless trees, all the same, so thick it was difficult to walk between them, rising high, so high that it was impossible to see where they ended.

A shrine. A small, dilapidated shrine, reclaimed by the forest. Moss and vines, peeling paint, cracked walls and caved in roof.

Tombstones. Unmarked. Abandoned. Temple remains, nothing more than a stone base marking where its walls once stood. Tombstones surrounded it on three sides, more tombstones than a human could count. Unmarked. Unloved. Forgotten.

I spin. Figures in the trees, growing in number. Darkness closing in. So many figures. Watching. Waiting. Afraid? Yes, they're afraid.

A body in the trees, swinging. Another body. To and fro, to and fro.

Running. The figures encroach. They're not engaging, merely watching.

A small girl's body, swinging from a branch.

Heartache. Despair. Too late. I'm too late. I'm so sorry. I cut her down and lay her body on the dirt below. No, it's not safe there. Under the brush until I can come back to help her. No time now. The figures, closing in. Run. Gotta run.

Too late.

She's before me. A shrine maiden. She sees me. Not Sayumi. *Me.* She smiles and reaches out. Her cold fingers caress my cheek, leaving burning in their wake. Her dead eyes sparkle.

"No!"

I let go of the brooch and it clattered to the floor. I grabbed my cheek; it was cold to the touch, like a burn. Wind chimes jangled in the distance. I ran to the door; the hall was dark and empty. The entire house was dark. I was alone. Nothing followed me back.

The chimes faded. I closed the door, locked it, and poured out more salt by the door and window, for what little good that might do. I put my gloves back on with shaky hands and picked up the brooch. The shrine maiden had Sayumi. Sayumi found the shrine, but something there had set her nerves on edge. The spirits in the trees weren't approaching it. They were... afraid of it? They were watching her, waiting to see what she would do, but Sayumi felt it too. She ran, and she found the little girl and cut her down. How did she even get up there in the first place? She was too small to reach a branch that high.

But then the shrine maiden found her, and she lost her brooch. Before I let go, before the vision cut out... I shuddered. The shrine maiden wasn't looking at Sayumi. She was looking at *me*. She knew I was there, watching, and there was a brief moment of… happiness? Like she was glad I was there.

The burning on my cheek faded and my heartbeat calmed. I knew what I had to do. It was the last thing I wanted, but it was the only option.

I had to go back.

22

THE NEXT MORNING I FOUND several messages on the work phone from Yasu.

"Hi, this is Yasu. Um, look, I've been having these dreams. About Keiko. She wants me to join her in some forest, but the thing is… I looked it up. It's a real place. They call it Kurohana. I'm sorry I keep calling, but I… I'm gonna go see her. I have to. I know, I know, it's just a dream, but it feels real. I'm just going to check. I'll let you know if I find anything, but maybe you can find something too. I dunno. Anyway, I'm gonna check it out. Bye."

"God dammit." Dreams weren't good. Yasu running off half-cocked into a haunted forest without knowing what he was up against was even worse. I dialled his number and waited. The phone rang and rang and eventually cut off. I tried again with the same results.

"Damn!" I slammed the phone back down.

Another complication I didn't need, and all because of his impatience. I told him I would keep him updated, and I told him I would find her. Why did he have to go and do such a stupid thing? He wasn't ready for what was in there; *I* wasn't ready for what was in there.

I grabbed my stuff and locked the door behind me. The shop would have to remain closed for the day. The few locals who dropped by could survive one day without their tea. There wouldn't be much of a tea store left if Sayumi didn't return soon anyway, so what did it matter if it was one day or even an entire week? Besides, I could use the opportunity to find Mrs Tamita's album as well. I looked up the emblem I saw on the school children's uniform and discovered it was two stops before Kurohana Station. The area wasn't familiar to me, but perhaps checking it firsthand would lead to some evidence of the album's whereabouts. Once I was done I would continue on to Kurohana. Two birds, one stone.

I ran to the station. Teenagers flooded the platform on their way to school. The train arrived and we piled in with barely enough room to stand. The pleasant, chilly air suddenly became hot and stuffy; heaters inside the train roared, working overtime, and the packed bodies weren't helping either. A few kids drew faces in the steam on the window glass; others chatted and played on their phones. Everyone was going about their life without a care in the world. I was just like them once. Until…

The train stopped and a few kids got out. I

grabbed the first available seat and sat down. A minute later it took off, swaying back and forth and tempting me to sleep. And yet, the closer the train got to Kurohana, the less populated it became. The carriage grew quiet, a sombre mood settling over the remaining few who were forced to travel past it each morning. The train stopped at Hirono Station and I stepped out. The air was brisk and chilly and hit me like a brick wall. The river from my vision was only a 10-minute walk from the station, if the map was to be believed. It was barely a river—a creek, really—so finding the area I saw in the vision shouldn't have been too difficult.

"Excuse me."

The station attendant looked up.

"Is there a small river or creek around here?"

He blinked a few times, as though I was disturbing his sleep, and then pointed over my shoulder.

"Sure, there's one just passed the parking lot. Why?"

"No reason. Thank you!"

He shrugged and went back to the magazine he was pretending to read while napping.

It didn't take long to find what I was looking for. It wasn't a new experience, but each time I stepped into a place I only saw in a vision for the first time it was like stepping into a memory. A memory that wasn't my own. I'd been there before, but it was my first time there. It was unsettling, like remembering a previous life.

But something was different this time. My memories of the creek had the banks covered in litter. The album was somewhere amongst that litter, but I couldn't locate it with all the interference. Now, however, the creek was clean. The banks were empty.

"Hey, wait! Excuse me!" Two school children ran by on the path beside the creek. They stopped and looked up at me. The emblem on their uniform was the same as the one from my vision.

"Hey, uh, this might sound a little weird, but when was the last neighbourhood cleanup around here?"

The two boys looked at each other, unsure if they should answer the crazy woman or run screaming all the way to school. One boy shrugged, and the other decided to engage with me.

"I dunno. A few weeks ago?"

A few weeks ago. My stomach dropped. The album could be anywhere.

"I, um, I'm looking for something that was around here. It was amongst the rubbish but it's gone now." They stared at me, unblinking. I couldn't blame them. I would too. "An album. A photo album. I don't suppose you know anyone who might have seen it, or where it might have gone? It's very important that I get it back. Very, very important."

The boys shrugged in unison and I sighed. I'd have to start again, if the album was even in one piece anymore. If it wasn't, my chances of finding it were slim to none.

"Did you say an album?" Another boy, walking by himself and dragging his bag along the ground, stopped beside the other two.

"Yes! A photo album! Have you seen one around here? Do you know where it is?" I let my excitement get ahead of me.

"Junpei was playing with one the other day," the little boy said.

"Playing with? What do you mean?"

He shrugged. "He found it over there." The boy pointed to the other side of the creek. "He thought it was a fancy book, but when he picked it up, it was full of photos so he threw it away."

My stomach dropped again.

"He threw it away… Where did he throw it away? Do you know?"

He pointed to some rice fields in the distance. My stomach fell into the abyss. They were huge.

"Some of the kids play there after school though," the boy continued. "I don't know if it's still there now."

The boy had seen the album. A friend of his picked it up from the creekside, played with it until he realised it wasn't what he wanted, and then threw it away in a nearby rice field. The boy didn't know where, exactly, but there was a chance that some other kids had come along and picked it up in the meantime as well.

I took a deep breath and stood up straight. I could grab the boy's hand, like I did with Hiroshi. Find the album that way, or at least clearer memories of it… I clenched my hand into a fist and shook my head. No. That wasn't who I was. That wasn't who I wanted to be. I wasn't going to steal memories from people, and especially not from children. I still had the photo of the album; if worst came to worst, I could try again with that, but there was still time to do a little more digging. It couldn't have gone too far. Nobody would just throw a family photo album away. It was full of precious memories.

"Thank you." I smiled, and the boys eyed me before running off. It wasn't the result I was after, but it was a start. I knew more than I did an hour earlier.

I walked over to the rice fields and worked my way around the edges. There was no rice growing, so it was easy enough to see, but there was no photo album either. If it was there once, it was gone now. I checked my watch and sighed. I would have to return for it another time. There was more important business to get to first.

Kurohana Forest was calling.

23

A FEW HIGH SCHOOL STRAGGLERS sat on seats and stood in the corner as I got on the next train. The train was quiet; a few typed on their phones while others went over homework they hadn't yet finished. Two more stops until Kurohana Station, and as we passed the first stop, the train suddenly fell quiet. Was it like this every time, I wondered? Did they somehow naturally sense how dangerous the area was?

"Hey, did you hear that they still haven't found Juri?"

"No way! Seriously?"

"Uh huh. Apparently the police have their hands full with so many cases that they haven't been able to dedicate much time to hers."

"Oh my god, that's gross. If they can't help, they should give it to people who can."

Two girls by the door started chatting as we approached Kurohana. The forest came into view and they scrunched up their faces.

"God, I hate that place. I begged my father to get me a scooter, but he was all 'you can take the train like everyone else!' Yeah, well, he doesn't have to go past *this* every morning, does he?"

"I know, right? It's so dark and creepy. I don't know why they don't cut it all down and turn the area into a park or something. No-one even goes there anymore. Apparently it's full of perverts."

"No way!"

"Uh huh. Yoshihiro was talking about it. Supposedly some girl was walking home and she was dragged into the forest by a gang of perverts. Nobody ever saw her again."

"Do you believe every piece of shit that comes out of his mouth?"

"What? Eww, gross. And no. But come on, look at it. Tell me you don't think perverts are hiding in that creepy-ass forest."

"I dunno about perverts, but I certainly don't want to go in there."

Neither did I. The train pulled up to the stop and I stood up. The girls eyed me and stepped away from the door, like I might drag them out and into the forest myself. I stepped into the cold air and a few seconds later the doors slammed shut. The train chugged off, the girls watching me with something I couldn't quite place in their eyes. Fear? Sadness? I'd rather go to school too then spend any more time here, I thought. This isn't my idea of a fun day either.

The forest took on a completely different atmosphere in the daylight. There was something eerie about it, ominous even, but it was… a forest. Trees. Greenery. It looked like any old forest. A family might come walking out of the trees and there would be nothing odd about it. A couple on a day out with a picnic basket might pull up in the parking lot and head in, laughing and excited about some time alone with nature.

And yet, it was cold. Almost unbearably so. It wasn't yet snowing, but it didn't need to. The dirt crunched underfoot, covered in a thin sheet of ice that had settled in the cold morning air. There would be no sneaking into the forest, that was for sure, but on the other hand, that meant nothing would be sneaking up on me, either. Nothing human, anyway.

A single car sat alone in the parking lot, an old brown bomb that looked like it needed to be put out of its misery. Yasu's? It had to be. No-one else would be crazy enough to be at the forest at this time of day… or ever.

I pulled out Sayumi's map. The station, parking lot, and *KUROHANA FOREST* sign were marked on the bottom. The trail I followed in the first time was a thin line that soon tapered off. About an equal distance after that, just off to the left, was the shrine. Before it, a river snaked perpendicular through the forest. If I found the river, I was on the right track. The shrine wasn't too far beyond that.

I walked over to the car and peered in, just in case. "Hello? Is anyone there?" No answer. The doors were locked and the ignition empty. Various papers were strewn across the backseat, as well as a lady's jacket. It was the fashionable type with the fur collar that I saw young women wearing all the time. Keiko's?

"Hello?"

Nothing. If it was Yasu, then he was already in the forest, and judging from the frost on the windscreen, he'd been in there a while.

"You fool."

I approached the path leading in, ice and dirt crunching underneath my boots. The red string was still tied to the tree, lying frozen on the ground below. My breath came out in short puffs of mist each time I exhaled. I rubbed my gloved hands together and picked up the string.

"Please don't snap."

It felt wrong to talk out loud. Like I was disturbing the forest and perhaps inviting unwanted attention my way. If they didn't already know I was there, they soon would. I knew roughly how far the string would take me, and what I would see on the way, but after that, I was blind. Taking one last look at Sayumi's map, I tucked it away safely in my pocket next to her brooch and Keiko's necklace.

"I'm coming, Sayumi. I'll see you soon. Wait for me."

24

STICKS SNAPPED LIKE ICE, AND every breath I took exhaled visibly in front of my eyes. The forest existed outside of time and space, or so it seemed with how bitterly cold it grew with each step. Tiny shards of ice hung from the string I left abandoned several days earlier, and every time I heard a snap I feared that was it; the string was finally broken. I was all on my own, nothing but ice on the ground and frozen trees rising high into the sky all around me.

Each footstep took me closer, but with it my apprehension grew as well. Sayumi was out there, waiting for my help, but she wasn't the only one. The shrine maiden was too, and she knew who I was now. She knew I would be coming for Sayumi and the other girls. Perhaps that was her plan all along. To draw me in to join them. I let out a breath and rubbed my hands together again for warmth. Not today. Today I would be leaving the forest with

Sayumi in tow, or I wouldn't be leaving at all.

I followed a familiar path, or at least as familiar as the path could be. The string lay where I dropped it, so all I had to do was pick it up and follow it in. Yet as I moved deeper into the forest, the hairs on the back of my neck stood on end. Not from cold, but from the distinct feeling that I was no longer alone. It was daylight, but it was difficult to tell. The forest grew darker with each step, like walking directly into night itself. In the corners of my vision, there was movement. Glimpses of shadows. When I turned there was, of course, nothing there. 'Just a figment of your imagination.' 'You're going crazy.' 'It's just the wind.' All those things people told themselves so they didn't have to believe the only explanation they knew to be true. The one explanation they didn't want to believe, or even in some cases, simply couldn't believe. 'Ghosts aren't real!' 'They only exist in the minds of the ill.'

Ghosts were very real, and they were just as dangerous as a flesh and blood person.

"I know you're out there," I called out. I stopped and turned. Nothing but trees, and a slight movement in the corner of my left eye. I turned to face it. "I'm not here to bother you." Nothing there. A chill ran down my spine and my ears prickled. Behind me this time. "I'm here for my friend and nothing else." Turning, I found myself face to face with a skeleton hanging from a tree. I screamed and fell back, landing awkwardly on the hard, cold ground. Pain shot up through my wrist and tailbone and the string, pulled too tight, finally snapped. I couldn't take my eyes off it. That skeleton wasn't there last time. Dirty, torn clothes hung like rags from its bones, but there was no flesh to speak of. It was a skeleton in human clothing, a noose hung limp around its neck.

I climbed back to my feet and dusted the ice and dirt off.

"If you're trying to get me to leave, I won't!" I screamed to no-one in particular. I spun around a few times, but I was all alone. Nothing but me and the skeleton hanging from the tree. The skeleton that hadn't been there a few days earlier.

I picked up the torn string and followed it to the end, my heart beating wildly and no doubt betraying the composure I was trying to keep. I didn't want them to know that they had spooked me, whoever they were. I didn't want them to assume me a threat. I just wanted to find Sayumi and get home. With Sayumi back we could work together on finding the other girls and stop more from disappearing, but alone I could do nothing.

The map said to continue forward in a mostly straight line. I would at some point come across a river, and once there the shrine would be a little further in, a smidge off to the left. If the shrine really was built on a power spot, then once I got closer I should have been able to sense it. *If* that was true, of course, and not merely a line the local government used to attract tourists.

My face grew numb in the cold, and it became difficult to see more than a few metres ahead or behind. The trees were thick, but so was the fog that hung in the air. Shadows constantly darted around in the distance, always on the edge of my vision and never close enough to grasp fully. They were watching me, that much I knew, but as long as they didn't engage, I didn't care.

I passed another skeleton hanging from a tree to my right. Like the other, this one also wore old, tattered clothes. They weren't modern in style, perhaps something worn in my grandparents' time. A farmer, by the looks of it. It swayed from one of the upper branches, too high for me to see in the mist, its feet at face level. The skull appeared to be looking down at me, pleading with me not to go on. 'This is what awaits you too. Go now, while you still can.'

I pushed through the trees, doing my best to continue in a straight line. It was impossible to tell; there was no sun to follow, no path, and no landmarks. I had to continue straight until I came across a river; I had to have faith that I wouldn't get lost.

A moan, long and drawn out, echoed behind me. I ignored it, pressing forward with my eyes dead ahead. They would not distract me from my path, for that would lead to certain death. Somewhere in the distance a wind chime rang out, and the moan stopped. I halted, dead in my tracks. The forest fell completely silent. Not a bug, not a bird, not even a whistle of the wind. The world was never truly silent; the background always held the hum of a TV, the buzz of a light, the breathing of a pet asleep in the corner, or a train passing in the distance. In that very moment, as I struggled to peer through the mist into what lay ahead of me, the forest was void of sound. There wasn't even a ringing in my ears, and every inch of my being screamed to run. It was unnatural, and evil, and *wrong*.

I opened my mouth, struggling with the cold and dryness. "H-Hello?"

A sound. My own voice, foreign to my ears, and then it faded away. The forest sprang back to life—whatever life it had—and continued on as though nothing had happened. Dirt crunched under my boots and a faint wind rustled through the trees. The moan was gone, but I wasn't alone. Far from it.

Another skeleton hung from the trees to my left, its clothes more tattered and torn than the last. A few minutes later, another to my right. They were like signposts, leading me in, while the shadows on the peripheries grew more numerous… and more restless. Somewhere in the distance I could hear the sound of running water, and my heart jumped. They were leading me forward, morbid signposts directing me towards Kurohana Shrine. I picked up the pace, shielding my face the best I could from angry branches attempting to claim warm flesh for themselves. Before long I found it; the river, trickling softly through the trees. It was almost serene. You could set a chair on the banks and read a book all day, losing yourself in the calming sounds of nature. If you didn't mind the bodies hanging from the trees for company, that was.

I ran through the water quickly, its icy cold depths reaching up to my knees. A skeleton, this time with just the tattered remains of shorts hanging from its hips, hung from a tree to my left, just barely visible in the fog. I ran towards it, picking up speed. Nearly there. I searched through the dense covering, looking for the next skeleton to light my path. Another, just beyond that tree. One more, over to the left. Then another, final body, this one without clothes at all, hung from a tall, sturdy tree. A structure rose in the distance behind it. A shrine gate. Behind that, visible through the middle, was a building, but not just any building. A shrine.

Kurohana Shrine.

I stepped through the fog and it seemed to retreat. The shrine gate rose high above me, parts of it crumbling but still holding out after years of neglect. The old shrine behind it wasn't in much better condition. Vines crawled up the walls, snaking through the windows and around the poles at the entrance. Part of the roof was caved in, and several sections of the main building appeared to be crumbling as well.

"Hello?" I called out. "S-Sayumi?"

Something sounded inside, like a rock being kicked along the ground.

"Sayumi?" I tried again, more confident this time. "Is that you?"

A figure stepped through the entrance. My breath caught in my throat.

"I've come to—"

It wasn't Sayumi. My heart dropped.

It was Yasu.

25

BAGS UNDER YASU'S EYES BETRAYED his exhaustion, while the cuts on his arms and face told the story of his journey through the dark forest.

"Yasu? Are you okay?" To say he looked like shit would be an understatement. He looked like someone had forcibly dragged him through the forest, and there was a good chance that was true.

Yet he grinned when he laid eyes on me. An almost feral grin that never reached his eyes.

"Oh, I'm perfectly fine now. I knew I could trust you to help. Now that you're here, everything's going to be just fine. We can finally be free."

Shadows lingered on the outskirts of the mist. I was expecting to find Sayumi here, not Yasu, and the confusion was evident on my face.

"What are you talking about?"

He took a step forward, and then another. He was in bad shape, pulling his left leg behind him with a slight limp. Blood stained his shirt and leaves stuck out of his messy hair. He wiped at a wound on his cheek, freshly cut and bleeding, and wiped it clean on his shirt.

"I mean-" he stopped in front of me and pointed to the right "-that we've been waiting for you."

I followed the direction he pointed in and my heart froze. A graveyard, old and untended. Full of moss-ridden, unmarked and toppled headstones, vines growing unbidden through them. So, it was true. The graveyard was real. Hidden behind it and to the left was the remains of a small temple, in even worse condition than the shrine, and to the right of that, a tree. It was one of the largest trees I'd ever laid eyes upon, so wide it would take three adults with their arms outstretched to reach around it. Branches poked out of the mist, and the longer I looked at it, the clearer it became. Now that it knew I was aware of it, it was like it stepped forth, large and imposing and proud, and made its grand entrance.

"We've been waiting so long." Yasu's voice choked, and then I saw them. Bodies hanging from the massive tree, like the skeletons that led me to the shrine. Like the girl Sayumi found and cut down. So many bodies, in various states of decay. I covered my mouth without thinking and took a step back. Yasu followed, pressing closer.

"S-She promised us," he said. "She said we would be free. She would set us free."

The necklace in my pocket throbbed. One body in particular hung from the lowest branch, swaying in the non-existent breeze. The necklace seemed to tug, like it wanted to jump free of my pocket and return to its owner. Even though I had only seen her in a photo, there was no mistaking it. Keiko was hanging from the tree, and by the looks of her, she had been there a while.

"Oh my god..."

"That's what she said."

Yasu's voice brought me back. His eyes flashed like crazy and the blood trickling down his cheek reached his lips. He wiped it away again, smearing blood across his face.

"What?"

"She said she would let us go. She would let us return, both of us. Keiko and I. Together. We could go back if we brought her fresh blood."

"I don't... I'm not..."

The shrine behind him buzzed with energy, and not all of it good. But the pull went beyond that, to the temple and the graveyard itself. The very area hummed with a haze of... excitement? No. Anticipation. The ground itself threatened to shake and tear free, unleashing its untold energy to claim what it long wanted.

Fresh blood.

"Who told you?" I asked. I took another step back, but too far and I would end up in the river. I needed to keep Yasu at a safe distance while I assessed the situation. He was crazed, and that made him unpredictable. I had to keep him as calm as possible for as long as possible.

"I think you know," he said. "You've seen her too, haven't you? She... she won't leave me alone." He smacked the side of his head a few times, his eyes closed in pain.

"The shrine maiden?"

He nodded, his eyes telling a silent story. A story of pain, of loss… of fear.

"Did she draw Keiko here?"

He shook and nodded his head. "No. Yes. Maybe. I dunno. Does it matter?" His voice broke as he screamed. "Keiko likes hiking, and she… and she…" Yasu scratched the side of his head furiously, drawing blood "…she could always see things I couldn't, you know? Like you."

I blinked and took another small step back. Not enough for him to notice I was retreating, not enough to cause him any further alarm. "Like me?"

"You can see ghosts, can't you?" He straightened up, rising to full height for the first time. "That's why I hired you, after all."

"You wanted me to find Keiko…"

He grinned and nodded. "Yes. Well, no. I mean, I already knew where Keiko was. Of course I did. We came here together, after all. It was Keiko's idea. She wanted to go hiking in the infamous Kurohana Forest. She'd heard stories from her friends that it was full of spirits and she wanted to see for herself." He turned to look at her hanging from the tree. "She just wanted to see with her own two eyes…"

"Yasu… Yasu, listen to me carefully." He turned back, his eyes glossy with tears. "When did you and Keiko first come here?" If I kept him talking, I could control the situation. For now, I needed him calm and cooperative. He was clearly unwell.

"I… I dunno. Time seems really funny here, don't you think? Haven't you noticed that? It's like day out there is night, and five minutes is five hours. How long? Four weeks? Five? Or was it less? I dunno…"

Four weeks. Yasu came to me less than a week earlier to find Keiko. She'd been dead for close to a month before that? Then that meant…

"It was supposed to be a brief hike. A nice, short walk. She wanted to have a look around and confirm for herself whether the rumours that the forest was haunted were true. I've never seen a ghost before so I agreed."

"What happened to her, Yasu?" I had to keep him talking. My eyes flickered over to the tree and I jumped. Keiko's eyes were open. She was watching me.

"I turned around, just for a second—it wasn't like I ran off or anything—but I turned around and next thing I knew, she was gone. It was just a second!" He was nearly crying. "I ran, and I ran, and I screamed out for her, but nothing. She was gone. Vanished into thin air. I had no idea where I was. I ran all day. Or all night, I dunno. But right when I was about to give up I tripped and fell into the river. I scrambled out on my hands and knees and when I looked up, I saw her. My beautiful Keiko…" He turned to look at the tree again. "Why would she do that? Why? We were so happy together."

I took another step back while his gaze was elsewhere. "I don't think it was Keiko's fault, Yasu. It's this forest. The energy here… the spirits… they're not good."

He turned back to me and grinned that feral grin

again. "I know." Only a few more steps to the river. I didn't know what my plan was once I reached the river, or even where I could go, but the waves coming off the shrine, the temple, the graveyard, and the tree all screamed danger. Not to mention the crazed man before me.

"She wanted Keiko. That's why she called her here. That… that bitc—" He closed his lips and forced himself to shut up. He covered his mouth, looking around in case someone heard him. He shook his head, stood up straight and started again. "The shrine maiden called her here, but in the end, Keiko wasn't strong enough. It was all for nothing. She took her from me, and for what? She wasn't strong enough, she said. But there were others who were. If I… if I brought them to her, do you see? I needed to get you here. Once I heard about you, what you can do, I knew that you were the one. She would be happy with you. Then she'd give Keiko back. We could go home. We could get married and live happily ever after, like she always dreamed of."

Another step back. I was just three steps away from backing into the river. I would need to make a decision, and fast.

"What do you mean, she wasn't powerful enough?"

He shrugged. "Why don't you ask her? I'm sure she'll be here soon enough. I've kept up my end of the bargain, now she has to keep up hers."

He was rapidly running out of patience, which meant I was running out of time.

"Where's Sayumi? Did she call her here too?"

He narrowed his eyes. "Who?"

"Sayumi. Ms Matsuda. The boss of Matsuda Tea and Sweets. How else did you find me?"

He shook his head in confusion. "I have no idea who that is."

If he had nothing to do with Sayumi, then where was she?

"I think this has gone on long enough, don't you? And please, stop backing towards the river. You're making me nervous." He tilted his head and smiled. "You didn't think I didn't notice, did you?"

"Yasu, you don't have to do this. We can leave, the two of us, together. We can take Keiko back. Give her a proper burial so she's not trapped here like the rest of them. We can free her, just like you said."

He shook his head. "There's no freeing the spirits trapped here. You of all people must know that. No-one can free them but the shrine maiden, and she won't free Keiko until I give her something better in return." He pulled out a rope he had been hiding behind his back. It was fashioned into a noose. "And that something is you."

26

I TOOK A STEP BACK and slipped, landing hard on the icy bank of the river. Yasu took the opportunity to lunge and sling the noose around my neck. I kicked and struggled, splashing freezing water over the both of us, but even in his emaciated and exhausted state he was too strong. The shadowy figures in the distance closed in, sensing that another soul was soon to join them. Yasu yanked, and the rope tightened around my neck. I gasped and grabbed for it, kicking and sliding on the icy ground.

"It's better if you don't struggle, trust me," Yasu said over the sounds of my kicking and choking. "It's painful, I know, but it'll all be over soon."

He dragged me past the shrine and through the graveyard towards the giant tree. Keiko's feet dangled above me and I struggled even harder. Dots swam before my eyes and my throat rasped. The icicles coating the ground made it difficult to get a solid grip, and my feet slid everywhere despite my best efforts.

Yasu was going to kill me. The shadows crowded around, the mist growing darker by the second. This was the show they were waiting for. Another to join their ghostly ranks, an eternity of loneliness that constantly hungered for more. They knew I could see them. They knew I would be joining them soon.

"Y-Yasu, no!" I managed to groan before he threw the rope over the lowest branch of the tree. He yanked, pulling down harder and harder, and soon my feet were dangling in the air. Keiko swung beside me in silence, two peas in a pod. She was like me, Yasu said. The shrine maiden called her here, and now she was stuck forever. Nobody deserved that, but as the black dots swimming before my eyes grew larger, I realised there were more important things to focus on. Like not dying.

"It's easier if you stop struggling." Yasu threw all his weight behind yanking the rope down, pulling me higher and higher. I couldn't reach the ground even if I wanted to, but at the same time, Yasu was exhausted. Something he mentioned earlier struck a chord with me; time seemed to work differently inside the forest. The first time I came here I noticed that as well. It felt like I walked its depths for close to an hour, yet when I arrived back at the station, the clock said only ten minutes had passed. If that was true, and Yasu left a message on the store phone last night saying he was heading to Kurohana Forest, how long had he really been here? Had one night for us been several nights for him?

Without food, without warmth, without shelter against the biting cold? No wonder he looked like death.

"Y-Yasu..." My fingers grasped at the rope around my neck, scratching and fumbling for any sort of leverage. Several nails were bleeding, and the smell of blood ('fresh blood' as Yasu so succinctly put it) was attracting more shadows by the minute. The mist remained dense, and the darkness grew even darker as more spirits joined the gathering. A live show. Exactly what they'd been waiting for all this time.

"Shh," he said. "Shh. You can see them, can't you?"

I couldn't answer, nor even nod in agreement. He looked around, on his knees and pulling down on the rope as hard as he could against my bodyweight.

"It's okay, you don't have to answer. I already know. I can't see them. Maybe that's weird to you, I dunno, but I *can* sense them. They're watching us, aren't they?" He laughed, followed by a hoarse cough. The rope jiggled, and I descended a few centimetres before he caught himself and yanked even harder. "Sorry about that. It'll all be over soon, don't worry. Your sacrifice won't be in vain. We'll say our thanks to you on the anniversary of your death each year. The anniversary of our freedom."

My eyes darted to Keiko, long dead beside me. Nobody was getting freed from here, and if I didn't do something, I would soon be joining her.

Something chimed in the distance and the forest fell quiet. The shadows froze, like all conversation between them suddenly ceased, and Yasu's ears pricked up.

"Do you hear that?" He looked up at me and a grin spread across his face. His eyes grew wide and he nodded. "Yes, yes, see! I told you! She promised! I told her I would bring you here! She's come, finally, she's come!"

The wind chimes grew louder, almost deafening. My hands, clawing at the rope wrapped tight around my neck, desperately wanted to cover my ears from the racket, but I was forced to endure it. Death was coming, in more ways than one. My fingers felt clumsy. They grasped, but it was more like a feeble attempt at brushing. My head pounded, and the chimes reverberated loudly in my ears. Yasu stood up, dropping me a few centimetres, and was saying something inaudible to a figure only he could see.

I was losing consciousness. One arm fell limp. The mist spread and withdrew, and the wind chimes faded into the background. A figure stepped forward, the icy ground beneath her feet undisturbed as she floated across it. She looked up at me and smiled. A smile I knew all too well. A smile that haunted my nightmares.

The shrine maiden.

Dirt stained the bottom of her red pants and appeared to grow up her legs like veins. The sleeves of her white top were torn, and the red threads woven through the outside of them dangled to the ground. The darkness extended up throughout her top, through her neck and up to her cheeks. It wasn't dirt staining her; it was darkness. It was evil.

"See, I told you I would bring you someone even

more powerful!" Yasu said, immediately dropping to a bow before her. My vision pulsed in and out. Sickness rose inside me and there was a loud ringing in my ears. It was impossible to tell whether it was the wind chimes or not, but the shrine maiden didn't even stop to glance at Yasu. She floated through the graveyard, the tombstones seeming to flee from her arrival, not a single one getting in her way as she proceeded closer to us. Her attention was focused entirely on myself; she didn't seem to notice that Yasu was there at all.

"Y-You promised you'd free Keiko," he said, looking up. He yanked on the rope once more for good measure. "Take her, she's yours. Just give me Keiko back."

He dropped his head in a bow once more. This was my last chance. Once the shrine maiden got her hands on me, it was all over, well and truly for good. The energy emanating off her was like nothing I'd ever experienced before; not even the storefront after dark. If the combined energy of the storefront was a magnitude four, the maiden in front of me was off the charts. The darkness that had tainted her spirit was overwhelming, growing stronger with each life the forest took.

She didn't care one iota for Yasu. He was a means to an end, and she never had any intention of 'freeing' Keiko. She wouldn't stop, either. Not with me, nor the person after me, nor the person after that. She would continue to consume souls, turning the forest into a spiritual black hole from which none could escape. In life she was a shrine maiden, the cleanest and most pure of all. In death she was tainted, a growing darkness that consumed all in her sight. What had happened to turn her into such a beast?

I kicked. I kicked with the last ounce of energy I had, willing to accept that it might be the last thing I ever did. My foot connected with Yasu's face and he screamed. It wasn't enough to knock him out, but he was exhausted and it was enough to get him to drop the rope. I hit the ground and adrenaline took over. I fumbled for the rope around my neck and threw it off.

The shrine maiden turned to me and screamed.

27

I COVERED MY EARS AND ran. My feet slipped on the icy ground and I tripped over several tombstones, but I pushed myself to get out of there as fast as possible. The shriek filled the forest, but that wasn't the thing that worried me most. On the outskirts of the mist lurked nothing but emptiness. Silence.

The shadows were gone.

If not even the shadows wanted to stick around, something told me that I didn't want to be there either.

Yasu got to his feet behind me, screaming and cursing. I turned back, slipping on the ground beneath me. He threw the rope down and started pointing and yelling. At me or the shrine maiden, I couldn't tell, but his finger waved in the air as his face contorted with rage.

"You promised! You said to bring her, and I did!" He stomped and slid, landing hard on his backside. "You promised!" He flailed on top of the ice, his voice hoarse.

The shrieking stopped, and he got back to his feet. I uncovered my ears. The shrine maiden was nowhere to be seen, but that only upset Yasu even further.

"Fine! I'll just do it myself!"

Yasu pulled a knife from his pocket and flicked it open. He pointed it at me and narrowed his eyes. The grin vanished from his face. Now only rage remained. Rage at the loss of his girlfriend. Rage at being lied to. Rage at the forest that had trapped him and forced him to do its bidding. He wasn't a bad guy, I thought while he waved a knife at my face from beneath the hanging tree. He was forced into a situation beyond his control and would do whatever it took to help the one he loved. If nothing else, I understood him perfectly. It did nothing to assuage the situation, however, and I scrambled back to my feet.

"I never wanted this!" His voice cracked. "Do you really think that I wanted to bring them here? I didn't kill any of them! It wasn't me! There's no blood on my hands, I'm innocent!" His eyes darted around the forest as he pleaded his case.

I backed up, tripping on a tombstone. It knocked the air out of me and I scrambled back to my feet, not daring to take my eyes off the angry man in front of me. "It's okay, Yasu. I understand. Really, I do." I held my hands out in front of me, trying to calm him down. Silence hung over the graveyard, and a quick glance around confirmed the spirits were still missing. Suddenly I felt very alone, and it left me disconcerted. Whoever would have thought that I'd come to think of them as company? They were trapped just as much as Keiko, or the other man's daughter, or even Sayumi or Yasu. But unlike Sayumi or Yasu, they couldn't leave. Jealousy was a powerful motivator for those unable to move on. They might be gone for now, but they would return, and soon. I had to act fast.

"I just want Keiko back." Yasu sounded as pathetic as he looked.

"I understand, Yasu. I really do. I'm here for the same reason."

He tilted his head, and it struck me how much he looked like a curious, confused owl, with his hair sticking up on end and covered in leaves and dirt.

"What do you mean?"

"I'm here for someone too."

Yasu lowered the knife. "Did she… did she take someone from you as well?"

I nodded and put my hands down. I was getting through to him. "She did. Someone very important to me."

"A boyfriend?" He whispered. He so desperately wanted someone to understand his situation. Good news for him; I did.

"No." I shook my head. "Not a boyfriend. My mentor. My… my best friend."

"Your best friend…" He scratched the side of his face with the knife and then pointed it towards me again. "Your best friend. How could you hope to understand the pain I feel? Keiko isn't just my 'best friend.' She's my life! I would do anything for her!"

I held my hands up again. He was reeling out of control, and right when I found something to pull him back. "I understand, I do! My feelings pale in comparison to yours, and she forced you to do such terrible things, I know! I know it wasn't you, Yasu. You never wanted to do such things!"

"No, I didn't!"

"The shrine maiden forced your hand. You didn't have a choice."

I backed up towards the shrine. I had no idea what awaited inside, or the state of it, but putting something solid between me and Yasu—just in case he went over the edge again—seemed like a good idea.

"No, I didn't."

"Nobody can fault you for what you've done." I almost wished the spirits would come back to take away the growing unease in the pit of my stomach. The quiet was unnatural and off-putting. Even the chirp of a bug or the slither of a snake across the ice would let me know that something else was out there, but there was nothing. Not even from the other side. "Anybody else would have done the same thing. I would have done the same, Yasu. I would have. I get it."

Would I? Would I have abducted girls and brought them to the forest if I thought it would save the person I loved? Innocent girls who had no idea what was going on, or the fate that awaited them after death?

"How many girls?"

Yasu tilted his head again. "I'm sorry?"

"How many girls, Yasu? How many girls did you bring the shrine maiden?"

He shook his head and shrugged. "What does

that matter? Two, maybe three. I dunno."

"Who?" I wanted to know. The girls' families deserved that much, and if I got out alive, it was the least I could do to help them.

"I don't know!" Yasu screamed, his rage flaring to life once more. "A little girl, I don't know! She was on her way to school and I grabbed her! She looked sad and alone, so I grabbed her, okay? And there was another, a teenage girl. She was walking home from work…" His face fell and he looked to the ground, the memories washing over him; the reality of the horrific acts he'd committed. "There was another. A woman at a convenience store."

My heart skipped a beat. A woman at a convenience store? Mr Fujita said his neighbour's daughter was discovered dead after going missing from a nearby convenience store.

"What happened to her?"

Yasu looked up. "Someone beat me to it."

I recoiled at his words. "W-What do you mean, someone beat you to it?"

He shrugged. "I thought she would be perfect. She was alone, it was dark, the number plates on her car were from a different prefecture. I thought she was just passing through on her travels. No-one would notice her gone. She was just the right age, too. The shrine maiden didn't seem particularly fond of the little girl." He stopped and looked up at Keiko, hanging still from the branch above him. "She seems to like them a little older." He turned back to me. "About your age."

I took another step back. I wondered if I could cover the distance between us and grab his wrist before he knew what was going on. If I could see the girls firsthand, and see the shrine maiden, I could see what Yasu was hiding from me.

"What happened, then? Why didn't you take her?"

He shrugged. "Like I said, someone beat me to it. I had my cloth ready, the car engine was running, all I had to do was run out and grab her as she exited the store. But as I was about to run, I noticed someone—a man—was with her, so I stopped."

"A man? Who? What did he look like?"

"I dunno. He had a cap on and got out of his truck. She didn't seem to know him though. I didn't stick around to watch either way. The next day I heard about you, the girl with the mysterious ability to find things, and I knew that you were it. You were the one the shrine maiden wanted. You were the one who would free Keiko."

Cap. Truck. My blood ran cold even as I watched my breath turn into mist before me.

Hiroshi. He wasn't just a stalker. He was also a murderer, and he was getting away with it because the police were too busy with all the other disappearances.

And I let him go. I had him in my hands, literally. The store itself even tried to keep him there. And I let him go. He was still out there, perhaps already attacking his next victim. What an idiot I was.

A mask settled over Yasu's face and he raised the knife once more. "We've done enough talking. You're stalling. For what, I don't know." He laughed. "We're in the middle of the forest. No-one will find us unless *she* wants them to, and when she comes back again next time, I'm going to make sure you're ready for her to take."

He leapt, his face distorted like a *Hannya* mask. I turned and fled towards the shrine just a few metres away. I slid on the rock floor, slick with ice, and turned the first corner I found. The inside of the shrine was exactly what I expected of it; crumbling, overgrown with weeds, and abandoned debris lying everywhere.

"You can't hide!" Yasu screamed from outside. "There's nowhere to go in there!"

He was right. The room I entered had no way in or out other than the broken door frame I came through. An old drum sat in the corner, a vine creeping up the side as though to play it itself, and on the other side of the room were a few scattered books. There was nowhere to go. I was trapped.

A scream outside pierced my brain. I covered my ears and backed up into the wall. It was not the shrine maiden's scream, not this time; it was Yasu.

"No! You promised! Go away!" His voice was close, just outside the entrance, but it was getting further away. "I did as you asked! I brought them all here! You promised me!" There was another scream, followed by footsteps on the ice. Yasu was running. "Leave me alone! Get away from me! Nooooo!"

The forest fell silent. I stepped away from the wall and listened.

Nothing.

I took another step.

No, not nothing. I swallowed.

CHAPTER TWENTY-SEVEN

Wind chimes.

28

HOW LONG PASSED WHILE I cowered in the corner? I held my breath and waited for the shrine maiden to swoop in and claim me, but she never did. Eventually, after what felt like hours (but was in reality probably only minutes) I stood on shaky feet and made my way back to the entrance. I feared the shrine maiden would be waiting there, that sneer on her face like she knew I would appear all along, but there was nothing.

I stepped outside and gasped. Yasu swung from the hanging tree next to Keiko, the rope he attacked me with looped around his neck. They were finally together again, just like the shrine maiden promised him. Together forever.

I was alone. Well and truly alone.

I had to find Sayumi. There was no more time to waste, and as much as I hated the idea—particularly from where I was standing—I knew what I had to do. Sayumi's brooch sat bundled in my pocket, covered and tucked in tightly at the bottom. I pulled it out and ran a hand over the cloth covering it. The shadows seemed to swarm out of nowhere, filling the mist around the shrine once more. I couldn't see them, but I sensed them. They were a safe distance—just in case—but the lure was too strong. Grab it. Go on. Unwrap and let yourself go. You can find her. You know she's here, it's just a matter of where. Do it. We'll even help you.

I checked the area one more time for the shrine maiden. I couldn't sense her and I had no idea where she had gone, or why, but there would be no better chance. Just for a moment. Just a quick look to see where she was. Then I would let go before anything could happen. The spirits knew I was there anyway, what did a few seconds of opening the door to their world and connecting it to mine matter? I could spend hours searching the forest for Sayumi and get nowhere. Days. Months.

Forever.

I dropped the cloth and clenched the brooch as tightly as I could.

All this time I feared what I would do without Sayumi's guidance. She pointed in the direction to walk and I followed. She pulled me back when I strayed too far off the track, and she shielded me when something came careening towards us, putting herself in the line of fire at my expense. She took me in when I had no-one else, gave me purpose, and taught me not to fear the gifts I had.

"Don't follow me."

When Sayumi left me that day, a day that seemed so many years ago now, I reminded myself that this wasn't an unusual occurrence and to think nothing of it. I knew how to run the store, I knew that if I kept away from the front after dark that all would be fine, and I knew that Sayumi would return when she was done. All would go back to normal.

And yet, there was one thing that I didn't know. Something I wouldn't realise until the world I'd grown comfortable in was ripped out from underneath me. I'd spent so long separating myself from it, isolating myself from the living because I feared the dead, keeping everyone at arm's length so the same thing wouldn't happen to them that happened to my parents. It took years to let Sayumi in, to relinquish the fear that one day I would walk in and find her drowning in her own blood in the middle of the room, much like I found my own mother.

Sayumi was never teaching me how to use my gifts. How could she? "You're the only person I know who can do such things," she once told me. "It's amazing. You don't just sense things, not like I do. You can *see* them, no matter where they are. You can feel them. You see what they see, hear what they hear. You remember what they remember, and you can differentiate all the different connections that make up the world. What you have is a truly special gift, Mako. I know it scares you. I'd be scared too. I *am* scared. I can't imagine what it's like to see the world like you do, and to have it see you back. But there's a reason you can, and you should trust in yourself. There's nothing to fear. You're not alone, and you never will be. Not anymore."

Not alone. Even when my parents were alive, I felt alone. After they were gone, I didn't know what to do. I feared my every touch would bring about the end. If anyone else got close, they would end up like my parents. I pushed everyone away when I needed someone the most, and Sayumi was the only one that kept trying. The only one who believed in me. The only one who trusted me.

She hadn't been teaching me how to use my gifts. No. She'd been teaching me to let go. To bring down the walls I'd built and let the darkness in. There were scary things out there, things waiting to pull me down into the depths with them. Tired, angry souls who wanted it to end. Fearsome, wrathful spirits with no desire but to see others join them in their pain. Scared, lost souls who wanted nothing more than to find the light again. I shut them all out. None of them would ever hurt me or my loved ones again. But I was no longer a scared, lost child. I was a woman, and the person most precious to me needed my help.

I let them all in.

I was in a box. No, not a box. The walls around me were wooden, but too large to be a box. Thin gaps in the wood allowed me to see outside. It was a building. A small building. A shrine?

Shadows surrounded me. Countless shadows, crying out in pain, pleading for help. They know I can hear them. They need help. They're lost and they want to get out. I can't help them. There's too many and I don't know where I am myself. How did I get in here? My head throbs. The little girl. Where is she? She was hanging from the tree. I cut her down and then… I push against the walls. Panic rises in my throat. Why won't the door open? There's barely enough room for me to stretch my arms out. My head hurts so much. Why won't they stop screaming? Is it night already? Why is it so dark? I peer through the gaps in the wood. A tree. There are several bodies hanging from it. Mist is rolling in. I'm so tired. Can barely keep my eyes open. Just a little nap. Then I'll…

They found me. Darkness swirled around my feet and a familiar tug pulled me down, dragging me into the nothingness where they would keep me forevermore. So many of them, more than I could ever hope to count. The souls of every spirit the forest had ever claimed, the souls of the unnamed and forgotten, buried in the temple graveyard, the souls the shrine maiden had summoned and kept trapped within her grasp. They all wanted free. They all wanted a piece of that light that shone within me, and as they clawed at me, scratching and tearing my skin, I screamed. It was not physical pain, but it was the most unbearable pain I'd ever experienced in my life. Like fire running through my veins, every nerve set alight, like being dunked into a pool of ice water, over and over again, no time to recover and more and more frostbite setting in. My limbs were being torn apart, ripped from their sockets as a million tiny hooks found their way into my skull and pulled in each and every direction. They were swarming me, an innumerable mass of pain and suffering, and I was to be another of their numbers.

"No!"

I screamed, and the brooch exploded in my hands. I hit the ground and looked around. I was back. They didn't get me. My hand stung like I'd grabbed hold of a hot poker and the flesh of my palm singed. On the icy ground below lay the blue stone that was once a part of Sayumi's brooch. I grabbed the cloth and bent down to pick it up; it was hot to the touch.

"What the hell?"

Sayumi was nearby, locked in an unknown shrine building. Before she blacked out she saw the tree. She was still alive. She had to be.

"Sayumi?" I called out. Spirits swarmed the area, circling me like a wary dog. They almost had me. They were in pain and they wanted out. I knew that much. They were all over me and I was nearly lost to them, but something broke the spell. Something broke the brooch.

I looked up. The shrine maiden floated in the air, smiling. Her hair whipped up like snakes in the air behind her, the black taint of corruption writhing across her clothes and her skin. The spirits howled in unison, a scream of pain and disappointment. They were so close, so very, very close, and they were being denied once again.

And then they were gone.

I ran.

29

THE VISION SHOWED ME THE tree Keiko was hanging from. I ran towards the only place the building could be and narrowly avoided colliding face-first with it as the fog lifted. I slid on the ice in shock and smashed into the wall.

"Sayumi!" I got to my feet and banged on the door. "Sayumi, are you in there?" She had to be. I saw her. The hanging tree was the right distance and angle away. "Sayumi!"

I took a step back, lifted my foot, and kicked the door. It took a few more attempts, but finally it burst open and I ran inside. Sayumi lay slumped in a corner, her eyes closed and her chest rising and falling with even breaths. She was alive.

"Sayumi!" I grabbed her shoulders and shook. "Wake up! I'm here! It's okay now, I'm here! Wake up!"

I pulled her into a hug, unable to stop the tears running down my cheeks. After all this time, she was here in front of me again. I was terrified and excited and relieved. A groan rumbled from her chest and I pulled back. Her eyelids fluttered, then finally opened, and her unfocused eyes glanced around the room.

"M-Mako? Is that you?"

I hugged her again, squeezing her as tight as I could. She coughed in protest and I let go. "Sorry. Are you okay? Is anything broken? Are you hurt?"

Sayumi shook her head, but her eyes remained unfocused and the look on her face suggested she was unsure of where she was. "What are you doing here?" She cupped my cheek, her eyes blurry.

"I came to find you. You've been missing several weeks now. I know you said not to look for you, but a lot has happened since then and—"

Sayumi's expression dropped. Fear crept up her face and panic flooded her eyes. She looked around frantically and grabbed my face. "Did they get you too?"

"Did who get me?"

She looked over my shoulder, out the open door. "They're out there. You can feel them, can't you?"

"The spirits?"

She nodded.

"Of course I can, but—"

She ran her hand over my face, checking my eyes like a doctor and pinching my skin.

"Ow, Sayumi, stop that. It hurts."

"We're not dead?"

I shook my head and patted her shoulder. "We're alive. You're safe. But if we don't get out of here, and soon, that might change very quickly."

"I don't remember what—"

"It's okay. We can worry about that later. First, let's get out of here."

I helped Sayumi up and stuck my head around the door. The forest was too foggy to see anything. I sensed spirits on the peripheries, but they were silent; watching and waiting. I had no idea where the shrine maiden was, but the forest was silent. That had to be a good sign.

As though reading my mind, Sayumi suddenly froze. "The shrine maiden."

"What?" I turned and Sayumi took another step back.

"The shrine maiden. She's out there. She's why… Mako! Did you see her?"

I nodded. "Of course. Several times now, but—"

Sayumi shook her head and backed up into the wall. "It's no good. She has us trapped here. We'll never get out. This is the only safe spot. She can't come in here."

I was growing more confused by the minute. "What do you mean, we're trapped? Why can't she come in here?"

Sayumi pulled me away from the door and closed it. "This here is a storage shed for the main shrine." I nodded, unsure of where the conversation was going. "She can't enter."

"Why?"

She peeked through the gaps in the wood towards the main shrine building. "Did you go inside the shrine?"

"I did."

"Did she follow you?"

"No, but… No. She didn't." Come to think of it, I heard the wind chimes and heard her drag Yasu off to the tree, and she knew I was inside… but she never entered the building. By the time I came out, she was long gone.

"Because she can't. Do you see? The forest corrupted her, but at heart she's still a shrine maiden. She can't step on hallowed ground. The graveyard and temple are tainted. Dirty. But she's a priestess. She can't step inside the shrine buildings and dirty them. They're clean and pure and need to remain that way."

Neither the main shrine building nor the storage shed seemed clean, but I didn't think Sayumi was talking about their physical nature.

"So, as long as we're in here, or in the main shrine, she can't get us?"

"Exactly."

"So, that's why you were in here."

She nodded.

"Okay. I get that. But… Sayumi, you've been gone a long time. It's been several weeks now. What happened? Why were you…" The words I were looking for escaped me. I indicated the corner I found her in. "Why were you asleep in here? It was like you were in a coma."

At that Sayumi shook her head. "I don't know. I don't even know how long it's been. Time seems to work differently in here." So, she noticed it too. "I was looking for someone. An old friend. I never found her, but I did find a young girl. She was hanging from a tree, and I was helping her down when…" When the shrine maiden appeared. I remembered from my vision. "I ran here. Or something led me here. I don't know. But when I got inside, it was like I couldn't keep my eyes open anymore."

"Do you think the shrine maiden did it?"

"I don't know."

"Can you sense her now?"

"No. You?"

"No. I think we should run."

"Do you know how to get out of here?"

"No. Do you?"

"No."

Well, that was great.

"We can't stay in here forever," I said. Sayumi nodded.

"We should run while we still have the chance."

"Are you feeling okay?"

She nodded again.

"Let's go."

30

WE WERE LONG PAST THE river before Sayumi spoke again.

"How long did you say I've been gone?"

"Close to three weeks now."

She fell silent as we trudged through the forest. The fog remained heavy, but Sayumi walked with purpose. There was no sign of the shrine maiden, and the skeletons hanging from the trees were gone. Gone, or we were taking an entirely different way out. It was impossible to tell.

"I'm sorry."

I shook my head. "It's okay."

"No, it's not. I wanted to deal with things on my own, like I always do. It was stupid of me. I should have trusted you enough to tell you what was going on."

"What *was* going on?" Our boots crunched on the icy forest floor in unison. Sayumi was not dressed for the cold, and she rubbed her arms for warmth.

"An old friend of mine from university went missing. I did a bit of digging, and the last time anyone saw her, she was buying a ticket to Kurohana Station. There have long been rumours that this forest is cursed, so I started looking into it. What I found suggested there might be some truth to those rumours, so I decided to check it out for myself. But I discovered one more thing. Something that I didn't want you to get wrapped up in."

My heart pounded in my chest. "What's that?"

Sayumi stopped and held a hand up. "Do you hear that?"

I stopped and listened closer.

"I don't hear anything."

"Exactly."

The forest had been eerily silent the entire time I'd been there. It didn't strike me as odd; not anymore.

"We're not alone, and yet they're leaving us be. Why is that?"

She was talking about the spirits. To that, I had no response. "I don't know."

Sayumi pursed her lips, did a full 360-degree turn, and then started walking again.

"When we get home, I'll tell you everything. I should have done that in the first place, and I'm sorry I didn't. I'm sorry for a lot of things. I know I told you not to follow me, but… thank you."

It was rare to hear those words coming from Sayumi. Usually it was the other way around. I was always thankful to her for everything she did for me, everything she taught me and everything she helped me with. Never once did I do anything that required her being thankful to me. I smiled.

"I couldn't just leave you be."

"How did you find me?"

I removed the remains of the blue stone from her brooch, wrapped safely in the cloth inside my pocket. Sayumi stared at it before tentatively picking it up.

"It's from your brooch. A man came to the store. Said he was looking for his girlfriend, and he heard I could help."

Sayumi raised an eyebrow. "Is that so? You're famous now."

I shook my head. "No, no. Not at all. I still don't know who told him about me. It's usually you who brings clients in. Anyway, I was looking for her, and that led me here. She was… hanging from the tree outside the shrine."

Sayumi mouthed 'oh' but said nothing. I continued.

"When I first came here, I found a girl. She was dead, lying under some brush. Your brooch was lying on the ground next to her."

Recognition lit up in Sayumi's eyes.

"I tried to keep your wishes. I really did. I ran the store, I tried to find that woman—the man's missing girlfriend—and I've been trying to find Mrs Tamita's family album as well. I'm getting closer on that. I did whatever I could to distract myself, because, to be honest, with each passing day I grew more and more worried that… you weren't returning." My voice trailed off. It was difficult to admit, especially out loud. I never was much of a talker, but Sayumi was all I had, and seeing her there in front of me again filled me with a myriad of emotions. One stood out above all the others though; happiness. She was back. All would be well again.

"Thank you for ignoring my wishes," Sayumi finally said. She gave a small laugh. "You know that we're not done here though, right?"

I nodded. "We need to put the shrine maiden to rest?"

Sayumi nodded. "This place has corrupted her. She never asked for it, nor could she fight it. But if we can help her, if we can set things right again... we should be able to help the rest of the spirits, too."

"Do you know what did it?" I asked. "What corrupted her?"

"I have some idea." She looked down at the blue stone and clenched her fist. "When we get home, I'm going to ask you to do something dangerous. Do you trust me?"

I nodded without a second thought. Sayumi patted my shoulder and smiled. A forced smile that she didn't believe in one bit and did little to make me feel better. I trusted her with all my heart. If she felt it was necessary, then I would do it.

We walked in silence for a while. I fought the urge to ask Sayumi all the questions swirling through my mind, so many questions that I didn't even know where to begin. Sayumi said we could talk when we got back. I waited weeks to find her, another few hours to hear her story wouldn't kill me.

Sayumi held her arm out in front of me and I walked into it. "What? What is it?" My eyes searched through the trees, fearing the shrine maiden was back. She was toying with us, letting us think that we could leave when in reality she was about to drag the carpet out from under us at the last moment.

"This way," Sayumi said, turning to the right. I followed her for a few minutes and then it hit me. The red rope on the ground. I recognised where we were.

The little girl's body.

Sayumi leant down and brushed the hair off her face. She closed her eyes and sighed.

"H-How long has she been here?"

Sayumi grabbed the necklace around the girl's neck and pulled. She put it in her pocket and looked around. "I don't know. Weeks outside might only be minutes here. Either way, she's been here too long. We can't exactly carry her back on the train, but at the very least we can let her family know where she is."

"Do you know her?"

Sayumi nodded. The girl's father was a store regular; of course Sayumi knew her. Sayumi knew everyone. I decided to tell her about the photograph later.

"Come on. It's not far now."

I looked down at the girl's body and said a quick prayer. It was the least I could do. "I know the way from here," I said. The spirits were still watching from afar. I didn't know what was keeping them at bay, but I had my suspicions. "We should go before the shrine maiden changes her mind and comes back."

I prayed to whoever was listening that she wouldn't.

31

BY THE TIME WE STEPPED through the broken back door to Matsuda Tea and Sweets, the sun had already gone down. I arrived at Kurohana Forest early in the morning. In my mind, I was within the forest's depths for a few hours at best. It was disconcerting. Sayumi looked at me when she saw the state of the door and I grimaced. "I'll explain later." There was a lot of explaining to do on both sides.

"Here, sit down." I led Sayumi to the break room, and she collapsed onto the couch. Her eyelids drooped and her shoulders sagged. "I'll make you some tea." I set about making a cup of her favourite: sencha.

"So, tell me about this man," she said. I jumped.

"W-Which man?"

"The one who asked you to find his girlfriend."

I sighed in relief. Yasu. For a moment I thought she meant Hiroshi, and I wasn't sure how she would handle that news yet, nor what she would do about it.

"There's not much to tell. Like I said, he came to the store and asked me to find his girlfriend, Keiko." I poured the water and let the teabag seep for a few moments. "He brought a photo and a necklace. I refused him at first. I didn't want to try it without you." At that, Sayumi looked up and smiled. I shrugged. "Anyway, I finally agreed and when I tried to find her, I saw the forest."

"Okay. And you don't know how he heard of you?"

I shook my head. "Maybe one of your contacts mentioned me."

Sayumi pursed her lips. "Perhaps. What happened to the back door?"

I scrunched up my nose. "Like I said, a lot of things have happened since you left."

"So, fill me in."

I told her about Hiroshi. His inappropriate comments each time he came to visit, the suspicions of the ramen waitress, the events of the night he broke into the house, and what happened when I grabbed his wrist. Sayumi raised her eyebrow at that and took a sip of tea as I gave her the cup.

"You grabbed his wrist and saw him standing in your bedroom?"

I sat down beside her with my own cup and nodded.

"Interesting. I mean, it makes sense. If it works one way, it should also work the other. I never thought of trying it like that."

I smiled like a child uncovering a hidden talent

their parent knew nothing of.

"But more importantly, are you okay?" she asked. She was calm; a lot calmer than I would have been if she had told me the same story.

"I am. I mean, I'm not physically hurt or anything. He never touched me, he just—"

"Broke into the house to get you."

When she put it like that… "Yes."

"Did you inform the police?"

"No."

She was contemplating what to say next, and I realised her hands were shaking as she raised the teacup to her lips. She was doing everything in her power to keep her emotions under control. I'd never seen her like that before. When it came to supernatural annoyances, Sayumi treated them as just that: annoyances. She never showed fear, never panicked, and stood toe-to-toe with more ghosts than I ever wanted to see in my entire life. But this was a human menace. In a certain way, he was far more dangerous than any ghost could hope to be.

"You said you would tell me about the shrine maiden." I hoped that by changing the subject she would forget about it, or at least calm down until we could do something about it. "You know who she is?"

Sayumi nodded and took another sip of tea. "She's my mother."

I choked on my own. "I'm sorry, your what?"

She tucked her legs up on the couch and held the teacup close for warmth. "Like you, I never had a lot of family, and I never knew my parents. I was raised in this very house by my grandparents, the owners of Matsuda Tea and Sweets before me." That much I knew. Sayumi never pestered me about my past, and I never pestered her about hers. She offered no information and I never asked. Now I understood why.

"My grandparents never told me much about my mother or father. I think it was too painful for them. They were my mother's parents. My father's parents lived on the other side of the country at the time. He was a good man, they said. A very good man. He loved his wife dearly, and he loved me dearly." Sayumi looked down into her tea and swirled it in the cup. "I would have liked him a lot, they said. He was tall and handsome and hardworking, and they couldn't have hoped for a better son-in-law."

"What happened?"

Sayumi continued swirling the tea. "Officially, he died from overwork. My grandparents said it was a broken heart. When I was three-years-old, my mother disappeared. She vanished without a trace and nobody ever heard from her again. My father pestered the police constantly to find her, and they tried for a while, but after weeks and later months of nothing, they gave up. The case remained open, but they had to put their resources into other things. Cases they were more likely to solve." Steam from the teacup rose around her face. "My mother was a shrine maiden before she met my father. She was the first and only priestess to work at Kurohana Shrine. It was there that she met my father for the first time, and when they decided to move the shrine into the village, she retired and married him."

Sayumi gave a small, sad laugh. "Less than a year later, I was born."

"I'm sorry…" Words failed me.

"My father left behind a diary," Sayumi continued. "I don't think my grandparents realised I had it, but I used to read it all the time. He noticed that my mother's shrine maiden garbs were dirty when he got home sometimes. When he asked her about it, she said she was visiting Kurohana Shrine. He asked her why, and she said she felt sad the adjoined graveyard wasn't being tended to anymore. With both the shrine and temple closed down, there was no more foot traffic, and with the graves being nameless, no-one to tend to them." Sayumi finished her tea and put the cup down on the table. "My mother was looking after the graves at Kurohana Shrine when she disappeared. She was caring for those spirits in the forest when no-one else would, and they trapped her there. All this time I had no idea, but when I saw her there…" Her eyes watered and she leaned her head back to blink them away. "I knew that was her. I've seen photos of her, of course, but instinctively I knew she was my mother. Whether she recognised *me*, however…"

Sayumi took the blue stone out of her pocket and held it before me. "This brooch was hers. My grandparents gave it to me when I entered junior high school. I wore it every day, hidden underneath my uniform. It made me feel close to her. A small piece of her right above my heart, like she was always there with me." She stopped and turned to me. "But it's not just connected to me. Remember when I said I was going to ask you to do something dangerous for me?"

She couldn't mean…

"You… want me to use it to find your mother?"

She nodded.

The stone in her hand was beautiful and glinted softly in the overhead light. Someone many years earlier laboured long and hard over that stone, and throughout the years it had been attached to two incredibly powerful women. One who was now dead, corrupted, and attempting to claim my soul.

"I'm not sure I can—"

"Do you trust me?"

I swallowed. "Of course I trust you, it's not that… When I tried to find you the first time, the shrine maiden looked at me, but she didn't just *see* me. When I let go… she was here. In the house. Just briefly, of course, then she was gone, but… she was right there in front of my face, and she smiled at me. She knew. It was the same thing that happened with my parents. She followed me back."

Sayumi nodded and presented the stone for me. "I know. That's exactly what I'm hoping for."

What exactly Sayumi was hoping for, I didn't dare assume, nor could I guess why she wanted to bring the shrine maiden to the house. It was our safe haven, and she wanted to bring that powerful spirit—her mother or not—into it? *"Do you trust me?"* That's what she said. I never had a reason not to trust Sayumi.

"Are you sure about this?"

"No."

I sighed. "If this goes wrong…"

"I'll be here," Sayumi answered. I hesitated a

moment—potentially my last—and pictured the shrine maiden in my mind as I grabbed the stone. Now or never. Let's end this.

I was back in the forest. Yasu was swinging from the hanging tree next to Keiko. Emptiness. The world was dark and difficult to see. Only the shrine stood out, a bright, shining beacon that both called to me and rejected me. Hungry. So hungry. Lonely. Dark. Cold.

The world spun. No way to tell up from down, left from right. Closing in. All around. Darkness. Panic. No air. Must stop them. Keep them away.

A wind chime rang. Its soothing ring washed over me and pushed the impending panic away. Yes, the wind chime. The one thing *they* despised. I did this for them and they did this to me. Now I will make them regret it until the end of time. Time that bends to my will, not theirs. Energy. So much energy, all around, but now gone. Need more. It's not enough. Too many of them. They will pay. Must find more.

The shrine dimmed. A rush spread throughout me. Everything went dark. Drowning… I was drowning!

"Mako!"

A voice, so far away. Not for me. For who? For her. Yes, for her. The one I need.

"Mako! Can you hear me? Come back!"

Such a sweet voice. There's power in it. A light. Precious light.

"Mako!"

Go.

I came back to with a start. I was lying on the

floor in the break room, Sayumi leaning over me. The lights were out.

"W-What happened?"

"Someone cut the lights. We need to get out of here. Now."

"Someone—"

Hiroshi.

He was back to finish the job.

32

"SAYUMI."

"What?"

She pressed against the door in the darkness, listening to what was happening outside.

"There's something I didn't tell you about the delivery guy." Something I was unaware of myself until a few hours ago. "Mr Fujita said his neighbour's daughter went missing. They found her the next day by the river, but… I think it was him that did it. Hiroshi. The delivery guy."

Sayumi looked at me in silence, frozen against the door. I realised she wasn't just listening, but keeping it closed at the same time. Human dangers were new to both of us, and something neither of us knew how to handle.

"The only way out is through the front," Sayumi said, her face turned to stone. The window in the break room was too high and too small for either of us to fit through. I fought the urge to force it anyway. Anything beat going through the front.

I shook my head. Sayumi remained expressionless, listening for signs of life on the other side.

"Mako!" A voice rang out through the house. "I know you're here. There's no point hiding." Sayumi's jaw set. She motioned towards the kitchen drawer. I shook my head again. She wanted me to grab a knife. The only knives in there were blunt—they'd be more effective at slapping than stabbing him—and if he was that close, it would all be over anyway.

I never realised just how much of a death trap the break room was. The door was the only way in, and after dark the only exit was the back door. The same back door Hiroshi was now guarding.

"I've been watching you for a while." He continued his tirade. "I mean, this is the perfect location. I see a lot of people in my job. Travel to a lot of different places. It's quite convenient. You get to learn the ins and outs of the city, and you get to know everyone's names, jobs, places of work… and otherwise." His voice got closer. Sayumi pushed harder against the door. "You learn when people are alone. So nice of Ms Matsuda to go on a trip and leave you here to run the store all by yourself." His voice turned singsong. Suddenly the door shuddered from the impact of his boot, and Sayumi let out a gasp.

"I dunno what you did when you touched me, you freak, but I do know one thing. This place is fucked up! All I wanted was a date!" Sayumi's eyes opened wide as another kick shook the door. I pushed myself up to my feet, but she shook her head. He already knew I was in there. It didn't matter if I was quiet or not anymore.

"You killed that girl!"

He laughed. "What girl?"

"By the convenience store!"

Silence.

"There are a lot of convenience stores and a lot of girls. I'm afraid I have no idea who or what you're talking about."

I strode towards the door, for a moment forgetting who I was talking to. "How many others did you kill? Was she the first?"

"Stalling, huh? Well, sorry to say, but I have no patience for your games today, freak. See, I just wanted to get to know you a little. Get a little closer, yeah? As soon as I saw this place, it was perfect. Quiet, unassuming, out of the way, and a pretty young woman running the register—all alone, no less. It's like god dropped everything neatly in my lap. I'm only here a few more weeks. My transfer is already in, so I'll be long gone before anyone notices that you are too."

The door cracked under his boot and Sayumi screamed. Hiroshi stood face-to-face with her, confusion in his eyes. He quickly recovered and stood up taller, puffing out his chest. "Ms Matsuda. Good evening. I wasn't aware you were home."

"What do you want?"

He snickered. "Well, I'm assuming you heard all that, so I think you know what I want. And I'm not opposed to two, if you catch my drift."

He stood head to toe in black with thick, heavy

gloves and a beanie pulled down over his face. The eyes and mouth were cut out. In one hand he held a rope, swinging it like he was at the rodeo.

"Get out of my house. Now."

"Oho, aren't you the feisty one?" He grinned. "I like them feisty."

He grabbed Sayumi around the neck, spinning her around and pulling her close. She struggled against him, but he was too strong. "Now, we're all going to play nice, and when I'm done, perhaps they'll be able to recognise both of you. If you don't, then you're going to be feeding the fish somewhere in the middle of a river. Okay?"

Sayumi threw her head back and connected with Hiroshi's nose. He let go and screamed, grabbing his bloody face, while Sayumi used the opportunity to run into the storefront.

"Sayumi, no!"

Hiroshi pulled his beanie off and threw it to the ground. Blood poured out of his nose. "Now you've done it!" He charged after her, kicking the door down. "Where are you?"

I skidded to a halt before the door. Hiroshi threw a bunch of papers and small gift items off the counter in his rage. "Neither of you are leaving here alive, do you hear me? And when I'm done, I'm setting this fucked up hellhole on fire! They won't even be able to identify your bodies in the remains!"

I couldn't see Sayumi in the dark, but every nerve in my body screamed *danger*. The entire time I'd been with her I'd never once seen Sayumi enter the store front. She feared it more than I did, and she didn't fear much, if anything.

"Get out here!" Hiroshi continued his rampage. The phone was just a few metres away. I remembered the last time he came to the house, how he had the line on hold the entire time. It wouldn't do any good. I needed to do something else, and quick.

The temperature in the room dropped. Icicles formed at the bottom of the window and slowly spread up. I could see my own misty breath. It was like being back in the forest again. Hiroshi stalked around the shelves looking for Sayumi. He pushed them over, sending bags of tea and snacks all over the floor, then wiped the blood from his nose again. It dripped to the wood below, landing with an almost audible splash.

The blood.

Oh no.

"Sayumi!"

Hiroshi turned towards me as a figure began to take shape before him. Several more followed it, morphing into a featureless human form.

"What the hell?"

Hiroshi stumbled over a shelf in his haste to escape the figure before him. He landed on his butt and scooted back towards the door. He reached up and jiggled the handle frantically. Sayumi emerged from the opposite side of the room and his eyes darted towards her.

"What the hell is wrong with you people?"

Sayumi didn't answer. A form materialised behind her, and her ears twitched in knowing. Another to her left, one more to her right. The others closed in on Hiroshi, who continued to fumble with the door. He grabbed spilt boxes of tea and tossed them, watching as they sailed through the air and straight through the dark shadows approaching him.

"Get away from me!"

Sayumi ducked through the shelves and skidded to a halt. Another shadow, much larger than the others, appeared a few steps in front of her. She took a step backwards, her eyes darting around, looking for another route of escape. A dark arm reached out for her throat and squeezed. Sayumi flailed, attempting to grab the shadow but her hands going straight through it.

"No!" I screamed and ran in. I had no idea what I planned to do, but I couldn't just stand by the door and watch her die. Not like this. Not after all we'd been through.

"G-Go!" Sayumi choked. I dove through the shadow and into Sayumi, sending the pair of us to the floor as she fell out of the shadow's grasp.

Darkness swarmed Hiroshi like a plague of zombies, covering him from head to toe, shadowy limbs groping and grabbing, pulling and tugging. His screams filled the room as he kicked and flailed.

"Are you okay?"

Sayumi rubbed her neck and nodded. Her eyes focused on Hiroshi and she grimaced as a wet tearing sound broke through his screams. They were feeding on him. Hiroshi pushed himself up the door, giving up on the handle and instead throwing his elbow into the window glass. Over and over he threw his entire body weight against it, but it was no use. He was bleeding from more than just his nose, and his attempts at fighting off his attackers were useless. How could you fight what you couldn‘t touch? He turned to us, fear in his eyes, and shook his head. Darkness dragged him to the ground and he screamed again. It was hard to feel bad for him after everything he'd done, but the sound of flesh being torn from bone didn't make me feel any better about the situation.

"We need to go."

Sayumi nodded, and I helped her to her feet. Her eyes grew wide, and I turned around. Another mass of shadows was forming, this time in our direction. They were standing between us and the door. Hiroshi gurgled at our feet. We were next.

Sayumi grabbed my wrist and pulled me behind her. We backed up into the wall; more shadows approached.

"What are they?" I couldn't keep the tremor from my voice.

"I'm not sure," Sayumi said. "They've been here longer than the house. Much longer. My grandparents warned me not to come here after dark. They said the spirits of war returned each night."

"War?"

The spirits were getting closer.

"Shirotama was the site of a bloody battle many hundreds of years ago. Many of the dead were buried in Kurohana Forest. Others were burned in mass cremations."

Sayumi pressed against me, her arms out to shield me from the encroaching darkness. It was right before us. She turned her head to the side, a wisp brushing past her face.

"They're the lost spirits of war." She grimaced. "They can't move on until—"

She stopped. The darkness before her stopped. I could hear no sounds coming from Hiroshi's direction, but there was something else.

Wind chimes.

She was here.

The shrine maiden had found her way home.

33

THE SHADOWS BEFORE SAYUMI RETREATED. Though they lacked form, I sensed one emotion wafting off them stronger than all the rest; fear. They feared the shrine maiden. It was her sacred duty to cleanse the unclean, to commune with higher spirits, and to drive away evil. The wind chimes heralded her arrival, and although they could not see her, like us, they felt her. Several shadows dissipated like mist. Others backed into corners to watch in safety from afar. The entire room sat balanced on the edge of a pin; one wrong move and the whole thing would collapse.

"She's here."

I peered past Sayumi's shoulder and, sure enough, the shrine maiden was standing by the front door, looking down at Hiroshi's body. He was gurgling; a wet, choking sound as his life drained to the floor below. He twisted his head and reached for the shrine maiden—Sayumi's mother. Sayumi put a hand by my hip and edged me towards the door. The spirits focused on the maiden, turning their gaze from us. This was our chance.

There was a hoarse, wet scream. Sayumi grabbed my wrist and we ran. She pushed me through the door into the hallway and slammed it shut behind us. The room filled with the sounds of ghostly screaming and I covered my ears. I had heard a similar sound only one time before; the night my parents were killed. The spirits were fighting, and the living did not want to be caught in the middle.

"Come!"

Sayumi grabbed my wrist again and we ran upstairs. I didn't know where she was taking me, but I followed. She opened the door to the spare room at the end and pushed me in.

"What the…" I'd never been in the spare room, and now I understood why. Sayumi told me it was where she kept all her rare and expensive items. I never had a reason to go in, and so I never did. But it wasn't just full of expensive items; talismans covered the back of the door, the walls, and even the roof. Cursive script adorned every visible space, illegible but clear enough in their meaning. This was Sayumi's safe room, just in case something ever happened to let the spirits in the storefront loose.

"Quickly." Sayumi pushed me to the middle of the room and forced me to sit. I was still taking it all in, but she moved to grab various items behind me. Downstairs grew silent. Was the room soundproof, or did something make the screams stop? Could the shrine maiden do anything to the spirits downstairs?

How did that even work? Her duty in life was to cleanse evil and drive it away, so was she able to do the same in the afterlife?

"What are we going to—"

Sayumi threw a bunch of items before me. Salt. An ink brush. Paper. Various sticks of incense. A lighter.

"Umm…"

She held a finger to my lips. A woman's laughter echoed throughout the house. That solved the issue of whether the room was soundproof.

"I needed you to bring her here for a reason."

"Okay…"

She grabbed a box of salt and poured it in a circle around us. "I need you to listen very carefully. We don't have much time."

I watched her as she finished the box and started again with another. "Okay."

"My mother, she—" Sayumi stopped to correct herself "—the shrine maiden, she wants power. That's why she's been seeking powerful mediums like yourself."

I nodded, but I didn't understand. Why me? I wasn't a medium. I merely saw things.

"The Kurohana Shrine used to be a power spot. The spirits there… the forest itself… it's very powerful. You've brought her here, but it won't be long until the forest drags her back, so we need to work quickly before that happens."

"What'll happen if she gets the power she's after?"

Sayumi threw the empty box of salt away and mixed some ink. "Then she'll be free. Once she's no longer confined to the forest, there's no telling what she'll do, but it won't be pretty." She stopped and looked up at me. "You of all people should understand what that means."

I nodded. "Sure." Bile rose in my throat. "What do you want me to do?"

Sayumi picked up the brush and grabbed my arm. She drew a character that took up the back of my hand, then drew further characters up both limbs. "You're going to exorcise her."

I laughed despite myself. "Me? Exorcise her? I don't… I've never… I'm not a medium, Sayumi. I'm not a priestess. What am I supposed to do? I've never done anything like this before! I wouldn't even know where to begin!"

She grabbed my other arm and continued. "I'll teach you. You'll be fine."

"Why don't you do it, then?"

She shook her head. "I'm not strong enough, and besides… she's my mother. If push comes to shove, I don't trust myself to…" She let the sentence trail off. She tapped the bottom of my chin when she was done with my arm and continued drawing characters on my neck and chest. It tickled, but I did my best not to fidget. "The evil in that forest corrupted her. The forgotten spirits of a brutal war fought long ago. Malice can take years to build. It stews and ferments until it finally spills forth and takes everything in its path down with it, and that included my mother. This wasn't her fault. It wasn't anybody's fault. None of them asked for this." She tapped the top of my head and I looked back down. She drew on my cheeks, my chin, my forehead.

"But we're going to help end it."

She put the brush down and grabbed a bowl full of water. Dipping some dried leaves inside, Sayumi splashed them on my face. She walked around the circle, chanting something as she splashed more around.

"You've done this before?"

"I have." There were so many things I still didn't know about her.

"Are you sure this is going to work?"

"I'm not." That wasn't confidence inspiring.

"So, those spirits in the forest, and the spirits downstairs… are they the same?"

She put the bowl down and grabbed the incense and lighter. "They fought in the same war, yes."

"Which war?"

"The war that lasted several generations. The war that united this land."

"Oh. I didn't know any battles took place here."

"Much of Shirotama's history has been forgotten." Sayumi wafted incense around the room. Sandalwood filled my nose.

"And the power spot? Is that… what is that?"

"Even more ancient than the spirits corrupting the forest. I fear they drew from its depths to become even more powerful, and that is how they claimed my mother."

"I see." I didn't—not really—but it was enough for now. Big war, angry spirits growing angrier for hundreds of years, dead shrine maiden, lots of malice all around. Got it.

"Are you ready?"

Wind chimes. Laughter floated down the

hallway, getting closer.

"W-Will that keep her out?" I pointed to the talismans covering the door.

"Not for long."

"Oh."

"We need to do this now. Just repeat after me." Sayumi started chanting in an ancient language I didn't understand. She said the words slowly, and I repeated them after her, one by one. My eyes fluttered to the door. The laughter was getting closer. Sayumi's voice rose, and I followed suit. She was repeating the same words. It was a chant, and we'd reached the beginning again. The second time around it came easier. I couldn't tear my eyes from the door, but as Sayumi spoke louder and more confidently so did I. Adrenaline coursed through my veins while my feet froze to the floor inside the circle of salt. My skin crawled and itched but I couldn't scratch it. I stared at the door, repeating the words Sayumi yelled. On the opposing side of the door, the shrine maiden was listening to us, and she wasn't happy.

The door shattered into tiny splinters, mere moments before I could grab Sayumi and pull her into the circle. The shrine maiden glanced at the torn talismans on the floor and stepped inside.

34

SEVERAL SHARDS OF WOOD SPLINTERED my skin, but I continued the chant. The blast shook Sayumi, but I remembered the words. I stared the shrine maiden down, repeating the mantra louder and louder in defiance. If it was a battle of wills she wanted, she'd get it.

Sayumi stirred beside me, rubbing her head. "The salt…" she muttered. Her fall broke the ring of salt around us. She turned towards the door. "Mother… I'm so sorry. I didn't know. If I had known you were there, I… I was just a child." The shrine maiden shifted her gaze to Sayumi and stepped closer. The talismans burned a trail as she walked through them. "I'm sorry you never had a proper burial. I didn't know you were there, and I was scared…"

The shrine maiden stood before us. I continued chanting the words, each round making my skin crawl like a thousand ants all over my body, biting and nipping and setting my skin ablaze. The maiden glanced down at me and the black veins crawling up her neck pulsed. They grew, spreading up throughout her face, and she turned back to Sayumi.

"No. Please, don't. I'm sorry. No!" Sayumi's voice filled the room as the shrine maiden fixed her gaze upon her. Sayumi grabbed at her neck like she was being choked by an invisible noose, her voice coming out in pained chokes. Squeezing her hand even harder, I focused all my energy on the shrine maiden. I knew the words. I could do it. Sayumi trusted me. She believed in me. I wouldn't let her down. It wouldn't end like this.

I repeated the words, louder and louder, until I could barely hear anything over the sound of my voice. The words took over like a mantra; I was no longer the one speaking them, they were speaking themselves. Sayumi's grip weakened with each passing moment. The shrine maiden—her own mother—was killing her, and there was nothing she could do to stop it. No doubt her mother brought Sayumi to this very house when she was born, introduced her to her grandparents, and perhaps even played in the same room we were sitting in. Happier times when she had a loving husband, a healthy baby girl, and their whole lives ahead of them. She was filial to her parents, but she never forgot her duties, even after she quit working at the shrine. She returned to the forest and continued to attend to the unmarked graves. The anonymous souls forgotten by time, but not by her. They deserved to be remembered, to be cared for in the afterlife, and Sayumi's mother did just that. Yet they claimed her all the same, took her from her family and warped her. Tainted her with their combined malice and corrupted her into the evil being trying to kill her own daughter before me.

Sayumi's grip on my hand weakened. Her body hit the floor, and I squeezed even harder. There was something hard inside her grip that fell into my hand. I let go and shifted my gaze from the shrine maiden for just a second. It was the blue stone. I turned back to the shrine maiden and smiled. I closed my eyes and squeezed.

When I opened my eyes again, I saw the shrine maiden in her true form. Webs of light snaked out from the stone, some reaching down to Sayumi on the floor, others towards the maiden herself. The dark veins visible to my naked eye ran much deeper in the spirit world, the corruption so deep that I wasn't sure if any of Sayumi's mother was left. Dark strands of her hair blew up in waves, and the air crackled and buzzed with energy. She turned from Sayumi to me and grinned.

I continued the mantra, not thinking about it but letting the words flow. I didn't understand their meaning, but I did understand their intent, and the sounds took on a life of their own as they left my lips. The shrine maiden floated towards me, a shadow blacker than the darkness itself, and every fibre of my being screamed to run, to get away as far and fast as possible. She didn't just want me dead; she wanted whatever it was inside me that allowed me to see things that others couldn't. Whatever it was that connected me to both worlds.

I thrust my hand forward and into her chest. I let

the fear melt away and instead embraced the rage bubbling deep inside. Rage at the pain the world had caused me. I embraced the sadness of my family lost, and the happiness of a new family found. I embraced all of it, let it wash over me as the chant surged out of my mouth, and finally, I embraced the power within that always frightened me. The power that let me see things I never wanted to see, and the power that brought forth the evil that forever changed my life. Not this time. No more running. No more fear. I was in charge. I was in control.

Tendrils snaked out of the shrine maiden, grasping for me like talons of corruption. They coiled around my neck, around my wrists, around my ankles. I shouted the words one last time, putting every last ounce of strength I had left into them. The shrine maiden got closer, her face mere centimetres from mine. She stared into my eyes, curious and unafraid. There was mirth there, perhaps even joy. She was not afraid. The attempts to exorcise her; the talismans, the incense, the holy water, the chanting, it was nothing to her. She was a shrine maiden. How could I dream of hurting her?

I embraced her, pulling her close. She struggled against me as I spat the final words out, the tendrils around my neck squeezing tighter and tighter in an attempt to deprive me of air and voice. I clenched the stone in my hand and the maiden screamed, her voice hoarse and otherworldly. She was bare to me, and I to her. I knew all I needed to know. There would be no more running. No more hiding.

As the final word left my lips, I smiled through

the pain. I had done it. I didn't know how, but I had done it. Her eyes widened, her grip on my throat unrelenting even as the darkness began to drain from her soul. She was so close, the finish line in sight and she did not want to give up, but it was too late. The darkness unravelled and confusion flickered in her eyes. I smiled even larger through the pain, my vision blurring.

"It's okay. It's over," I choked.

She screamed, an ear-shattering shriek that pierced my eardrums, and the room exploded into white. I hit the ground and the tightness around my neck faded away. The burning sensation across my skin dissipated and the frigid coldness in the air snapped. Warmth returned, and gradually, so did Sayumi's mother. The darkness melted away, the veins of corruption retreating. Her inner light returned, filling the room with her purity. The effort drained me of what little energy I had left and I fell to my hands beside Sayumi. As the last of the darkness drained from her feet I looked up. A beautiful woman stared down at me, confused and seemingly taking in her surroundings for the first time. Her eyes widened when she saw Sayumi and she dropped to her knees beside her. She pressed a hand to Sayumi's cheek and whispered something I couldn't hear. Sayumi moaned, her hand grasping for the source of the voice. Relief washed through me. She was still alive. Thank god. The maiden then turned to me.

"Thank you."

I opened my mouth to say something but then closed it again. There was nothing to say. She clasped her hands around mine; around the blue stone I was still holding. It beat like a heart inside my hands, reacting to her touch. She smiled at me a moment, expressing everything she wanted to say with her eyes, and then turned to Sayumi. Sayumi pushed herself up, rubbing her head and groaning in pain.

"Ugh… What happened…?"

The blue stone stopped beating.

I smiled.

The shrine maiden was gone.

35

I PRESENTED SAYUMI WITH SENCHA in the cherry blossom tea set I kept for her return. Several days had passed since the events with her mother and, while there was some bruising around her neck, she was otherwise fine. Physically, anyway.

"How are you feeling?" I asked. She picked up the teacup and admired it.

"Where did you get this?"

"It came in while you were out. I thought you'd like it, so I put it aside for you."

Placing a hand on my arm, she smiled. "Thank you. It's beautiful." She took a sip of tea and closed her eyes.

"What are you working on?"

Books lay strewn across her desk that looked older than the house itself. Half were open and spread across every spare space while the rest towered high in the corner.

"I'm trying to dig into the history of Kurohana

Forest. I thought that if I uncovered what really happened there, and those involved, perhaps we could appease the spirits. Let them finally move on."

We had helped Sayumi's mother, and with her gone the disappearances had stopped. We visited the little girl's father the next day and Sayumi delivered his daughter's necklace in person. His cries rang through the closed screen door as Sayumi told him in private what happened. My heart sank. But while Sayumi's mother—the shrine maiden—had passed on, the other spirits continued to linger. The forest was still dangerous.

"Do you really think we can help them?"

"Honestly? I don't know. My mother tried for so long, and in the end they took her with them. We can't let that happen to anyone else, and if there's a way to allow them to move on, we have to try. They're angry and lost. They didn't ask for this, just like my mother never asked for it. Sometimes bad things happen, and we're the only ones left who can deal with it. Oh! While you're here." Sayumi bent down and rummaged through the bottom drawer of her desk. "I have something for you."

"For me?" The surprise in my voice escaped before I could hide it. Why would she have something for me? She handed me a small box about the size of my palm.

"Open it."

I tore the paper off and opened the box. Inside was a bracelet with a shining blue stone. I looked up.

"I don't..."

"It's yours now," Sayumi said. "I received it from my mother. It was all I had to remember her by. Now I'm giving it to you."

"Sayumi, I can't—"

She placed a hand on my arm again. "After my parents died, my grandparents were the only family I had. After they passed, I had no-one. It was just me and this big, empty, haunted house. But the more I thought about it, the more I realised that that's not entirely true. I do have family left. I have you."

Flustered, I could do nothing but smile. She took the bracelet out of the box and put it around my wrist.

"T-Thank you." They were the only words I trusted to come out.

"And if I ever go missing again, well, you can use that to find me quicker, hey?" She smiled. It was a joke, but the meaning behind the gift wasn't lost on me. We had both lost our families. We were both alone, burdened by a similar past and similar gifts that kept us separated from the public at large. But we weren't alone. We had each other.

"Do you think your mother is okay now?" I asked. "Did she… move on?"

Sayumi leant back in her chair and took another sip of tea. "I think so. I hope so. But the funny thing is that since she left… I can still sense someone here. I don't know if it's her, or…" She shrugged. "Anyway, I should get back to this. The sooner we can figure this out, the better. Thank you for the tea. Oh, and the electrician will be out tomorrow to check the house, although something tells me he's not going to find anything wrong with the wiring." She smiled. "The repairman should be out to fix the door before the weekend as well."

I nodded and stopped by her door on my way out. Behind Sayumi stood two figures. They looked down at her, smiling, and I realised I had seen them somewhere before. Hiroshi's vision. They were in my room the night Hiroshi broke in. They attacked him with the pen. The same two faces stared back at me from the photo on Sayumi's bedside table. They turned in my direction and smiled before fading away. They were still watching over their granddaughter and her family.

Family.

I smiled and returned downstairs. The store wouldn't run itself.

After the events with Sayumi's mother, Sayumi called the police chief personally to come around to the store. They were old friends and, she said, the only one who would believe her when she explained why there was a dead, mutilated man lying on the floor of a tea and sweets shop. He took care of things, and a few days later called to tell Sayumi there was enough evidence to connect Hiroshi to the murder of Mr Fujita's neighbour's daughter. They found hair and DNA, in addition to fingerprints at the scene that matched. "I'll take care of it," he said, and that was the last we heard of him.

That wasn't the end though. There was still one

problem left. Mrs Tamita's family album. I sat at my desk with the photo before me. Now or never. I grabbed it and closed my eyes.

I felt the usual pushing and pulling of energy leading me in all directions, but I blocked out everything that wasn't the album. Colours swam in and out and before long I was standing in a rice field. A farmer bent down and picked the album up. He took it to his storage shed and closed the lock. I let go and smiled. It was still there. I grabbed my stuff and ran downstairs.

"Where are you going?" Sayumi called out after me.

"I found Mrs Tamita's album! I'll be back soon!"

The train rocked and shook, mirroring my excitement. I flew down the stairs and made my way over to the rice fields. Two boys ran past me, chasing each other by the water. I knocked on the door and a familiar face greeted me. It was the farmer.

"Hi! It's a little sudden, but my name's Mako and I'm looking for this." I showed him Mrs Tamita's picture of the album. "Some children said they saw it nearby and—"

"What? Oh, the album! Yes. It's in the shed out back. I found it in the fields a few days ago. I was wondering how it got there. It looked important, so I didn't want to throw it away. Come. I'll go get it."

I went with Sayumi to return the album to Mrs Tamita. Her face lit up when she saw it.

"Oh my! You found it! You really found it!" She held it close and took my hand. "Thank you, dear!

Thank you. How can I ever repay you?"

I shook my head. "I'm just glad you have it back now." She didn't need to know how difficult it was to locate, nor the ghostly figure of her husband I saw along the way. He stood in the corner as we said goodbye, only this time, he was smiling.

Two days later, Sayumi knocked on my door. Somehow I already knew what she was going to say. "Mrs Tamita passed away last night." Her husband knew. He feared that her concern over the album was so great that when she passed, it would keep her on earth, her business unfinished. *Quickly.* The word echoed in my head once more.

I picked up the photo when Sayumi returned to her room and closed my eyes. Threads of colour pulled me here and there, but I couldn't find Mrs Tamita, nor her husband. The album sat in pride of place on her mantel, her oldest daughter crying on the sofa nearby. They were gone. Both Mrs Tamita and her husband had moved on.

I found the album in time. I opened my eyes and tore the photo up.

"Mako! Someone's here to see you!" Sayumi called out from the storefront. I put my cup of tea and magazine down and stuck my head around the corner.

"Hmm?"

A familiar smiling face greeted me beside an unfamiliar one. My face lit up.

"Megu!"

"Mako!"

I ran into her arms and let her envelope me.

"It's been so long! How are you?"

She held me at arm's length and looked me over. "It's a long, long story. You look well. And—" she peered over my shoulder and waved at Sayumi "—I see I'm too late, as usual. Hi, Ms Matsuda!"

"Hi, Megu." She smiled. "Lovely to see you again." She shifted her eyes to the woman beside her. "Who's your friend?"

"Oh, uh, this is Aya. She's… my friend." Megu let go of me and rubbed her hands together. "We heard Mako was having some troubles and thought we'd come to help. Aya is a… or can release her… I dunno how you say it, what did you call it again?"

"Ikiryo," I said. Sayumi raised her eyebrows.

"Oh. Well, I can't say I've ever met a person who could do that before. Welcome!"

The young woman she called Aya looked around the room and shifted closer to Megu.

"I can see ghosts," I said with a smile. "She can too." I pointed to Sayumi.

"I can turn on a computer!" Megu punched me on the shoulder with an awkward laugh and then withdrew her hand just as quickly. "Sorry. I'm the useless one, I know."

"You're not useless," Aya and I said in unison. Megu sheepishly grinned.

"Anyway, it would appear that our help is no longer needed? I feel kinda silly now, rushing all this way…"

I pulled her into another hug. "You're always

welcome here, Megu. Always. You're family, after all."

Sayumi stepped out from the counter and rested a hand on my shoulder. "Why don't you girls go catch up. I can cover out here."

When was the last time we were all together like this? Warmth spread throughout my chest and I smiled despite myself. I wasn't alone. Not anymore.

WANT EVEN MORE?

Also available in *The Torihada Files*:
Kage

Kowabana: 'True' Japanese scary stories from around the internet:
Volume One
Volume Two
Volume Three
Origins

Toshiden: Exploring Japanese Urban Legends

Reikan: The most haunted locations in Japan

Read new stories each week at Kowabana.net, or get them delivered straight to your ear-buds with the *Kowabana* podcast!

ABOUT THE AUTHOR

Tara A. Devlin studied Japanese at the University of Queensland before moving to Japan in 2005. She lived in Matsue, the birthplace of Japanese ghost stories, for 10 years, where her love for Japanese horror really grew. And with Izumo, the birthplace of Japanese mythology, just a stone's throw away, she was never too far from the mysterious. You can find her collection of horror and fantasy writings at taraadevlin.com and translations of Japanese horror at kowabana.net.

Made in the USA
Las Vegas, NV
04 February 2023

66812942R00135